THE
VEIL WEAVERS

THE
VEIL WEAVERS

MAUREEN BUSH

www.coteaubooks.com

Edited by Barbara Sapergia
Cover designed by Tania Wolk
Printed and bound in Canada

Library and Archives Canada Cataloguing in Publication

Bush, Maureen, 1960-
     The veil weavers / Maureen Bush.

(Veil of magic ; bk. 3)
ISBN 978-1-55050-482-8

I. Title. II. Series: Bush, Maureen, 1960- . Veil of
magic ; bk. 3

PS8603.U825V43 2012   jC813'.6   C2011-908524-0

Library of Congress Control Number 2012932998

· 2517 Victoria Avenue
Regina, Saskatchewan
Canada   S4P 0T2
www.coteaubooks.com

10 9 8 7 6 5 4 3 2 1

Available in Canada from:
Publishers Group Canada
2440 Viking Way
Richmond, British Columbia
Canada   V6V 1N2

Available in the US from:
Orca Book Publishers
www.orcabook.com
1-800-210-5277

Coteau Books gratefully acknowledges the financial support of its publishing program by: the Saskatchewan Arts Board, the Canada Council for the Arts, the Government of Canada through the Canada Book Fund, the Government of Saskatchewan through the Creative Economy Entrepreneurial Fund, the Association for the Export of Canadian Books and the City of Regina Arts Commission.

For Mark, Adriene and Lia,
who actually enjoy the idiosyncrasies
of living with a writer.

CONTENTS

CHAPTER ONE

TRICK OR TREAT

J OSH," MOM CALLED FROM THE KITCHEN, "could you and Maddy get the pumpkin ready?"

"Sure," I yelled. The biggest, ugliest pumpkin we'd ever carved was waiting in the hall. I carried it out to the front steps while Maddy bossed me about where to put it.

We'd carved it to look like Gronvald the troll, the scariest thing we could think of for Halloween. Small eyes and wide slanting eyebrows framed the stem of the pumpkin, turning it into a fat, crooked nose. His mouth opened in a bellow, wide on one side but twisted tight and low on the other.

Once Maddy and I agreed on the perfect spot to set the pumpkin to scare everyone coming up the walk, I lit a candle and placed it inside. It looked just like Gronvald.

A crow glided into the garden and landed on the sidewalk, black against the fresh snow. There were always crows watching me, now. He inspected the pumpkin and then hopped away with a sharp caw. He must have recognized Gronvald.

Last summer, after Maddy found a green stone ring, we'd discovered a magic world separated from the human world by a veil of magic. The ring, the nexus ring, made it easier for magic folk to travel between the worlds. But each time it crossed the veil it left a hole, a tear in the veil, and magic was leaking out.

Gronvald had used the ring to steal gold in the human world; gold was all he cared about. Aleena, a water spirit, loved the ring too. It made it easier for her to visit back and forth between worlds, and she liked to torment Gronvald by keeping it from him. They both desperately wanted the ring back, but we fought to get it to Keeper, the giant at Castle Mountain, who smashed it so it couldn't damage the veil again.

While we were in the other world I'd absorbed a lot of magic. Maddy doesn't have any but Keeper says she doesn't need it – she just fits in naturally. I'm the odd one, except it feels perfectly normal to me.

We left the crow on guard duty and headed to the upstairs bathroom to get Maddy into her costume. She pulled her long blonde hair into a ponytail while I got out the face paint. As soon as I started I could feel magic, only a flicker, but at least it was still there. I drew a hairline in a vee down her forehead, and made it look like fur by drawing thin lines in shades of brown. Then I drew a dark triangle on her nose, and lined her eyes with black to make them look round and dark. When I was done, I handed her the fur hat and fake-fur cape she and Mom had found at a thrift store.

Maddy was dressing as an otter-person, but no one else knows about them so we told people she was an otter. Because she's only eight, Dad was taking her halloweening. I was meeting friends from my grade seven class, if I could transform myself into a crow. At least I was thin and not too tall, and I had shiny black hair. The mask I'd made would cover my freckles and pale skin.

Once Maddy was ready, she ran downstairs to help Mom with the Halloween treats, and I went to my room and started a drawing. As I worked, magic flowed through me. This was the only time I could feel magic in the human world, when I was making art. I loved it – it made my work so much better, and it helped me feel connected to the magic world, a reminder we hadn't imagined it. Soon Gronvald glared back at me, nasty and snarling.

The doorbell rang. "The first one!" Maddy called out. "I bet it'll be a really cute little kid." I could hear her follow Mom to the front door and plunk down a bowl of candy. Then Maddy yelled, "Josh, you have to see this."

I ignored her and kept drawing.

"Josh! You really need to come!"

I sighed. "Just a sec." I put down my pencil, and walked down the stairs.

Maddy stood near the front door, staring past Mom. I stopped beside her; my mouth slowly opened. Two otter-people stood on our doorstep. Not kids dressed as otter-people, although that would be strange enough. Real otter-people. Greyfur and Eneirda had come to call.

MOM REACHED INTO THE BOWL OF HALLOWEEN candies, grabbed two handfuls and held them out to the otter-people. "Where are your bags? Do your parents have them?"

The otter-people stared at her with round, dark eyes. Behind Mom, Maddy shook her head and held a finger to her lips.

I stood there, stunned. What were they doing here? What if Mom realized they weren't kids?

When they didn't answer, Mom said, "Well, hold out your hands."

Maddy held out her own hands, palms up and touching to form a bowl. They copied her, and Mom filled each pair of cupped hands with little chocolate bars and boxes of raisins.

"We want to talk to them, Mom," said Maddy, pushing past her.

"Great costumes," Mom said as she headed back to the kitchen.

I squeezed past Maddy and moved them to the far end of the porch, away from the house light. I couldn't believe Mom thought they were kids – no one could make costumes that good.

They were exactly what Maddy was trying to be, part human, part otter. Their fur reached down their foreheads towards their dark pointy noses, and gleamed in the light in a way that Maddy's face paint never could. Their eyes were round and almost black in the shadows. Their mouths and ears were small, their feet flat and wide at the toes.

Greyfur was a little taller than me, with deep brown fur shading to grey on his head and across his shoulders, and amber skin on his face and hands. Eneirda was smaller, about Maddy's height, with auburn fur and soft tan skin.

Maddy and Eneirda greeted each other, Maddy's small hand reaching out to touch Eneirda's four fingers. Eneirda smiled as she studied Maddy's costume.

"What are you doing here?" I whispered.

"You must come with us, *tss*," said Greyfur, his voice deep and firm.

"Shhhh!" I said, too loudly. I lowered my voice. "If anyone looks closely, they'll see you can't possibly be kids. So speak quietly. Please!"

Greyfur nodded and continued in a softer voice.

"Giant at Castle Mountain sent us. You must come to Gathering. Tears in veil are not healing. *Sssst!* You must help."

"Keeper said they'd heal," I said, shocked.

"They are not," said Eneirda. "Tears are getting worse. *Sssst!* Magic is leaking."

No! I thought. *No!* Humans caused enough damage, through changes so large they reached into the magic world, like mines and tunnels and even rising temperatures. Holes in the veil were extras the magic folk didn't need.

"What can we do?" I asked. "Why do you need us?"

"Maddy because she sees clearly. Josh because he is... Greyfur struggled for the right word. "*Tss.* Because he is strange."

What?

Greyfur shook his head and tried again. "Josh has magic that is unusual. *Sssst!* Our magic is not...it is not enough. We hope Josh's will be."

Magic was strong in me the last time I was in the magic world, but I had no idea how to fix the tears. I felt confused and a little scared by what they wanted from me, but desperate to help, too. "I want –" I glanced at Maddy. "*We* want to help, but we don't know anything about healing the veil."

"Nevertheless, you must come," said Greyfur. "We will wait until you are ready, *chrrr*."

We stared at each other. For a moment, Greyfur

reminded me of Keeper, solid and immovable.

Eneirda said, "Giant at Castle Mountain sent for you. *He* believes you can help." I could tell she wasn't so sure.

"We have to try, Josh," said Maddy, in her most determined voice.

We have to try, I told the knot in my stomach. I nodded. "Wait for us in the garden. We need to get ready."

"*Chrrr*," purred Eneirda. "We will wait." As they walked down the porch steps they paused at the pumpkin.

"Come on!" I hurried them into the garden. "Stay in the shadows," I whispered, as a group of witches and wizards turned up our front walk.

Quickly, they slipped into the darkness where the porch light doesn't reach.

MADDY AND I RACED INSIDE.

"Layer up in your warmest clothes," I said. "Long johns, heavy socks, a warm shirt. Warm pants – not jeans. Are you wearing your ring?"

She lifted her hand so I could see her silver band, the elven ring Keeper had given her when we brought back the nexus ring.

I nodded. "Hurry." I dashed into my bedroom,

yanked off my clothes, and pulled on warmer layers. We were going back to the magic world! I felt a wave of joy and then I immediately felt guilty. The tears weren't healing – and I had caused some of the damage, although I hadn't meant to. I could still feel what it was like when magic was strong in me, when I could breathe the world. I would do anything to protect it.

I ran through a mental list as I leapt down the stairs. Winter boots, fleece, jacket. Hat, mitts. What else? Firestone! I needed my firestone!

I spun around and raced back up the stairs. I pulled open a drawer and groped under my T-shirts, sure I'd hidden it there. Finally I found it, snug in a back corner. It looked like an ordinary black stone, a smooth, flat oval. I slipped it into my pocket and ran downstairs.

As I joined Maddy at the back door, I glanced out the window – three crows were sitting on the fence. They seemed restless, shifting back and forth, watching the house. Waiting for me.

"Josh is going to take me," Maddy announced as Dad picked up his jacket.

He paused. "Are you sure?" He looked disappointed.

"Yes," I said. "We want to go together."

Maddy zipped up her jacket over a fleece, and flung her cape over her shoulders. I was pretty sure she wouldn't want to keep wearing a fur hat, so I grabbed a red wool hat and shoved it into my pocket.

Dad hung up his jacket. "Okay. Be back by eight.

And don't go too far."

I nodded, but didn't say anything. We'd be going much further than he could imagine, and be gone for much longer. But we could cross time when we crossed the veil, and be back before Mom and Dad knew we were missing.

Dad handed us pillowcases for the candy we wouldn't be collecting. "Watch out for trolls," he said. "And ghosts and goblins and, well, whatever's waiting out there."

Maddy shivered.

I struggled not to. "We'll be fine," I said. "C'mon, Maddy."

AN ALMOST FULL MOON WAS RISING, HUGE AND orange in a deep blue sky. The crows circled overhead, dark against the moon.

As we walked past the gate, Eneirda and Greyfur studied the Halloween treats in their hands, puzzling over them. Maddy giggled and held out her pillowcase.

"Humans," muttered Eneirda, as they dropped in their candy. But she smiled when Maddy grinned back. They walked together, talking quietly.

"Where are we going?" I asked Greyfur.

"To the creek, *chrrr*," he said softly, as we passed a group of small creatures with their parents.

It was the perfect night for Halloween – maybe too perfect. It felt eerie, walking down the street to the park with an escort of crows.

"Did you come for us because your magic is stronger on Halloween?" asked Maddy.

"Of course not," said Eneirda. She used her "humans are so foolish" voice. "Because of costumes. Only now can we safely walk in city, *hnn*."

Still, magic seemed stronger to me, maybe because the magic folk were near. It felt like the magic world was a little closer tonight.

Greyfur and Eneirda walked swiftly, straight north and then down into Confederation Park, away from the houses and streetlights and kids in costumes. We didn't have far to go. The otter-people led us to the stone water fountain that drained into the creek. Then they stood, waiting.

"The crows will open doorway," said Greyfur.

"I can do it," I said.

"No. *Tss*. It is arranged. Your magic must be preserved."

I shook my head in frustration. Opening doorways never tired me like it did magic folk. But no one ever believed me.

The crows circled the pond below us. I could feel their restlessness again, a need to hurry that was edging into irritation.

I heard voices and saw a human couple walking

through the park. One crow followed them, a second continued circling the park, and the third, the smallest, returned to us.

She landed on my shoulder, looked at Maddy and trilled in what sounded like laughter. Eneirda smiled and turned her head away.

"What?" asked Maddy.

"*Chrrr.* She thinks your clothes are funny," said Eneirda, struggling to hold back a laugh.

I glanced down at Maddy. Her otter costume suddenly looked silly, like we were little children pretending to be powerful magic folk.

Maddy slipped off her cape and I helped her wipe off the face paint. The little crow perched on a low branch and watched, head tilted to one side, as if we were putting on a show just for her. We filled our pockets with Halloween candy, and hid the cape and our pillowcases in the bushes near the creek.

Once the couple had left the park, the other crows joined us. They lined up on the grass and began to mutter softly. Slowly, mist formed. It was hard to see at first, white against the snow, but gradually the mist thickened, obscuring the trees and pond beyond it.

A doorway opened in the mist, and Eneirda pushed us forward. Maddy and I walked into a fog so thick I could see nothing in it. The mist thinned and we stepped into the magic world.

CHAPTER TWO

THE ROCKIES AT DAWN

VEN IN THE DARK I COULD FEEL THE difference between Calgary and the magic world. It was both brighter and darker, with no city lights, a gazillion stars and a luminous moon. This world was rougher and wilder than the human world, with a power I could feel deep in my body. Maddy and I grinned at each other. We were back!

Greyfur, Eneirda and the crows followed us through the doorway, and immediately conferred with Corvus, a large crow with white-tipped wings who was waiting for us. According to Keeper, crows don't like to talk to not-crows, so one crow is always chosen to speak for them all. This was Corvus.

A boat rested on the bank of the creek. It was like

the one we'd travelled in last summer, bark stretched over an oval ring of branches. We all climbed in, the smallest crow perching on the edge of the boat beside my shoulder.

Their paddles were magical and could travel upstream or downstream with equal ease, but tonight the otter-people were working extra hard, paddling in a fast, smooth rhythm as if they were in a hurry.

We followed the creek down a deep, treed valley, and crossed a marsh alive with the rustling of animals and the fragrance of mint and mud. A wolf howled as we slipped around a beaver dam. When Maddy shivered, I pulled her close to me.

She watched everything through the engraved silver band Keeper had given her. When I borrowed it, I could see magic strong and golden on Eneirda and Greyfur, and on the boat and paddles. It flashed off the wings of the crows and glowed softly on everything.

The stream carried us down to the Bow River. As soon as the boat slid into it we could feel the power of the current. Eneirda and Greyfur murmured to their paddles – the boat turned and we headed upstream.

The crows continued their patrol. Gradually more crows joined them, until they were an inky black cloud.

Greyfur grumbled. "We do not need so many crows. I told Corvus. But all of them want to be here. All of them want to escort their Crow Boy. *Sssst!*"

He frowned at me like it was my fault. I flushed.

The otter-people didn't like it that Maddy and I were human or, I guess, that the crows liked my magic.

As the moon rose high above us, the temperature dropped, and cold seeped in. When Maddy's teeth started chattering, I said, "We're getting really cold. Could you warm us with magic?"

"You do it," said Eneirda.

I frowned. "I don't know how!"

"We cannot spare magic," said Greyfur. "You must do it, *hnn*."

I looked into his face and saw a fatigue I hadn't noticed before. Eneirda looked the same – pale, dark around the eyes, and tight-jawed with the effort of paddling. "Why are you tired? I thought your paddles were magic."

Eneirda leaned close to Greyfur and hissed, "*Sssst!* Tell him."

I don't think she meant us to hear, but sound carries well on the water. "Tell us what?" I said.

Maddy glanced at me and leaned forward to listen.

Greyfur shook his head at Eneirda and spoke. "Our magic is weakened by magic leaking, *tss*. This journey is difficult for us."

"*Sssst!*" hissed Eneirda. "Tell them all."

Greyfur sighed. "As magic leaks out of our world, we are weakened. We ate muskberries to build magic, as many as we could. *Tss*. Now we hope we are strong enough to reach Castle Mountain."

"That is why," Eneirda added, "you must warm yourselves."

Maddy slipped her ring off her finger and looked through it at Greyfur and Eneirda. "Josh," she whispered, "you can see their magic fading."

I held up her ring. The magic that had radiated off Greyfur and Eneirda so strongly was paler now, and thinning in spots. So I decided to try. My magic had weakened in the human world; now, as I concentrated, it flowed faster, filling me. I imagined myself surrounded with magic, and immediately felt warmer.

Greyfur had been watching – he nodded his approval.

"What about Maddy?" I asked.

"*Chrrr*. Maddy too," he said.

"How?"

"Wrap her in magic."

I took a deep breath, determined to try. I pulled magic into my hands and drew it around Maddy, imagining a bubble of warmth. Maddy made a face but sat still as I experimented. Magic began to flow, and slowly I surrounded her.

She relaxed as the magic warmed her, but she frowned at me. "You have too much magic," she said. "It's not right for a human."

But I loved it, and so did the crows. They circled closer above me, as if they could feel my magic.

"*Tss*. Humans used to have magic," said Greyfur.

"Really?" asked Maddy. "What happened?"

"They became busy with other things, *hnn*, and forgot."

"And now it's gone." Maddy sighed. "Except for Josh."

"Not gone. Out of reach for most humans. *Chrrr.* There is always magic, even in human world."

"There is?" Maddy asked, her eyes shining.

"Yes. *Tss.* Think about it."

Maddy sat pondering. Then slowly she smiled and started a list. "Art. Music. Babies."

Greyfur nodded. "Birth."

"And death?" she asked, hesitantly.

"Of course," said Greyfur.

"Then," she said, hesitating again as she thought about it, "why does it matter if magic leaks from your world to ours?"

Eneirda hissed, and the crows cawed.

Greyfur just nodded. "There is more magic here, *hnn*. You feel it?"

We both nodded.

"When magic leaks from our world to human, *tss*, we have less. That harms us."

"We care for magic," said Eneirda. "Humans waste theirs. *Sssst!* So we have much. And they have little."

We were all silent after that, deep in our own thoughts. Eventually I slept, lulled by the rocking of the boat.

I woke as the boat ground onto gravel, coming to a stop in total blackness.

"I can't see a thing," said Maddy.

"*Humans*," muttered Eneirda.

"Do you have your firestone?" asked Greyfur.

Of course. I reached into a pocket and pulled it out. I held it in my palm, smooth and black, and let magic fill me. Slowly, gold threads within the stone began to glow. I focused more magic into it, and the stone cast enough light for Maddy and me to see as we stepped out of the boat onto a pebble beach.

The wind was sharp, and it was hard to hear anything over an enormous roaring. Even with my firestone, I couldn't see beyond the edge of the river and a small pocket of beach. Either clouds had blocked the moon, or we were somewhere the moon couldn't reach, somewhere narrow and dark and cold.

"Now we wait for dawn, *hnn*," said Greyfur.

"We just wait?" asked Maddy. She sounded nervous in the dark.

"Would fire comfort you?" Greyfur asked.

"Oh, yes!"

While Maddy built a teepee of small dry twigs on the shore, I focused on my firestone, studying the gleaming gold threads. Gently I reached in and grasped the tip of one. I pulled it out and touched it to the kindling as it twisted and flared. When the wood began to smoke I dropped the thread onto it. As the fire grew, Maddy carefully added larger twigs and then small branches.

We warmed our hands, and turned and toasted all our cold spots. Sparks from the fire rose straight to the stars. But I could only see stars above us – to the sides we were enclosed in darkness.

Slowly the sky high above us shifted from black to deep blue. We were on the pebbly bank of a river, the Bow, I assumed, surrounded by cliffs and forest, on the outside curve of the river where it turned after plunging down a waterfall.

Eneirda and Greyfur stood at the edge examining the water flow – where the water was deep and fast, where it was slower. With dismay I realized they were choosing a route. They turned to us and nodded. It was time to go.

My stomach felt like it had its own waterfall, plunging and smashing and gurgling. I reminded myself that the otter-people's boats were amazing and their paddles strong with magic, but I wasn't convinced. Greyfur and Eneirda looked more tired than I'd ever seen them.

Maddy studied them through her ring. "Their magic is thinning. They need to rest a little longer."

"No," said Greyfur. "We must go now. We will rest at Castle Mountain."

When Maddy looked ready to argue, Greyfur held up a hand. "Waiting will not help, *tss*. We will become more tired. We must go now."

The crows circled close overhead, squawking angrily as we settled in the boat.

"What's wrong with them?" I asked.

Greyfur said, "They do not trust what they call our infernal boat to keep their crow boy safe. *Tss*. But we will."

I closed my eyes for a moment, searching for courage. Then I swallowed and helped Maddy into the boat.

Eneirda and Greyfur muttered softly as they pulled magic into the paddles and headed up the waterfall. They propelled us through the crashing waves and around huge jutting rocks. The paddles sang as they followed the deepest flow of water, weaving back and forth across the width of the river. Maddy and I hung on as the water fought back, tearing at the boat. When we finally reached the top, we sighed in relief. Greyfur and Eneirda sagged with fatigue.

"I can paddle," I said.

"No!" said Greyfur. "Your magic must be preserved." They sat up and continued paddling, slowly but steadily, ignoring their fatigue.

I could feel the approval of the crows, still driven to push on.

As the mist cleared, mountains appeared high above us, pale in the early dawn. All the colours were soft pastels, white and blue, pale gold and soft red. It would be beautiful in the human world. Here, with the glow of magic on everything, it stopped my breath. Then I remembered we were going to a Gathering so I could try to repair the veil. I felt sick.

Greyfur and Eneirda drooped lower and lower, pale and panting. Then Eneirda collapsed, slumping over her paddle.

"You can't do this," said Maddy.

"*Tss*, we will do what is needed," Greyfur muttered.

"For how long?"

"Until it is done."

"Until you die?" Maddy demanded.

Eneirda lifted her head for a moment. "If we complete our task..." and then she shrugged, as if that was all that mattered.

"I'll paddle," I said.

She started to shake her head, then paused "*Tss*. Perhaps you could try," she said, sounding both distrustful and hopeful. She shifted to sit beside Maddy, while I moved forward. Corvus circled low, cawing.

"He does not approve," said Greyfur.

"That's enough, Corvus. I'll be fine," I said, as I picked up the paddle.

Greyfur said, "Let magic flow through your hands."

I could feel the grain and the strength of the wood. As I dipped the paddle into the river, it bit deep and the boat surged forward.

The river snaked back and forth down a wide valley, the water a sparkling blue. Splashes of gold lit the riverbank as the last aspen leaves clung and spun in the wind.

"There's Castle Mountain," I said, pointing with the blade of my paddle. The rising sun lit Castle in an orange glow, highlighting all the fissures in the mountain, with snow lying in bands like a layer cake.

When we finally reached Castle I breathed out in relief, but Greyfur steered us to the mouth of a small stream.

"Where now?" Maddy asked.

"The Gathering is above the lake behind Castle Mountain," said Greyfur.

"You need to rest."

Greyfur just shook his head.

We paddled up the stream, and as it grew smaller, the boat became smaller too. We shrank with it, becoming as small as the stream twisting around a maze of fallen trees. The crows were huge, flying high above us. I felt odd, constricted, as I struggled to paddle into the tangled forest.

Maddy watched through her ring. "You're pulsing," she said. "It's like your body wants to be bigger but magic is holding it in." She examined her own hand, Greyfur and Eneirda, and the boat. "Magic is flowing from Eneirda into the boat so it can keep us small. And more magic is flowing from you and Greyfur into the paddles."

The stream wound through a forest of lodgepole pine, lichen hanging silvery grey from dead branches. When we reached a waterfall I stopped in shock. How could I paddle up that?

But almost immediately we were rising up the waterfall, Greyfur digging his paddle in at the front of the boat. I leaned forward and joined him. If we took turns, we could keep it moving straight up, although I noticed it surged forward more for me than it did for Greyfur.

Finally the stream calmed as the ground levelled out. With a moan, Greyfur slumped forward, exhausted.

"Rest," I said. "I can do this." I could feel my body stretching as we grew and settled back into our normal sizes. Paddling felt no different, but my body felt better, like I could breathe fully again.

I kept going, up the stream to the lake. All kinds of creatures were gathered at the far shore, waiting for us. With an escort of crows cawing above us, I paddled towards them. I felt deeply afraid.

CHAPTER THREE

THE GATHERING

THE CROWD OF MAGIC FOLK WAITING FOR us seemed to grow larger and larger as we crossed the lake, a mass of beings shifting in and out of the shadows. I dug in and paddled faster, driven like the crows. Greyfur and Eneirda were totally still.

The crows circled above us and began to caw in a raucous announcement of our arrival. Every creature waiting for the Gathering turned to look. I could hear the crows' pride, but I just felt embarrassed.

"Corvus," I said quietly, and shook my head.

Corvus cawed once and the crows fell silent. But they still flew overhead in a mass of black.

Otter-people were waiting as we reached the shore. Shaking with exhaustion, Greyfur and Eneirda struggled to stand. The otter-people caught them, helped them from the boat and carried them to a small encampment on the shore of the lake, away from the others.

I borrowed Maddy's ring to watch. The magic that had surrounded them earlier was almost gone. What was left was thin and pale. Everything else around me glowed with magic, but it seemed to fade above the lake. That's where I spotted a doorway in the veil, with a ragged gash stretching across it. Golden light poured through into the human world. All around it, the magic world looked faded and grey.

The crowd of magic folk spread out along the lakeshore, staying far from the tear in the veil. They stayed away from me, too. I felt alone in the huge crowd, with only Maddy at my side. Well, Maddy and the crows, but they weren't exactly a comfort. Corvus landed on my shoulder and cawed. The others settled around us, a coal-black honour guard.

I looked more closely at who was here for the Gathering. Moose and deer grazed in the meadow near porcupines, chipmunks and marmots. Two buffalo stood at the edge of the meadow. Mountain sheep perched on the cliffs above the lake.

Aleena sat on the shore, far from the otter-people. She looked like a shadow, in a black cloak with long grey hair shading to black down her back. She raised a hand in greeting but didn't join us. Although she was a powerful water spirit, she looked pale and afraid.

Maddy pulled me over to her. "Come with us," she said.

Aleena stepped back and shook her head. "No!"

"I thought we were friends," said Maddy. She sounded hurt.

I saw something flicker over Aleena's face, but she didn't speak right away. Then she nodded towards the magic folk. "I am here because of you and Josh," she said, "and the need to repair the veil. *They* are not my friends."

I remembered how much they disliked her for her part in damaging the veil. "Stay here," I said, "away from the crowd."

Aleena nodded, and Maddy waved as we walked away.

When we'd first known Aleena, we'd fought her and Gronvald for the nexus ring. He still hated us for destroying it, but Aleena had helped, when she finally understood what the tears were doing to the magic world.

We'd become sort of friends when I'd rescued her and Maddy, after we were pulled deep into the earth and trapped. The earth magic made Maddy and Aleena really sick, but I'd loved it, so I took the nexus ring deeper still so that Maddy and Aleena would be allowed to leave.

But I understood her uneasiness with the magic folk

at the gathering. I wondered who else was uncomfortable with the crowd. As we walked back, I looked into the forest. I thought I spotted bears and wolves and strange creatures I wasn't sure I wanted to see too closely. Some moved deeper into the shadows when they saw me watching. I could feel their simmering energy – I did not want to be at the centre of it.

As we studied the crowd, a large hand came down on my shoulder.

"Keeper!" Maddy yelped as I turned.

He hugged us both and laughed. "I knew you would come," he said, his voice deep and rumbly. He looked just the same as the last time we'd seen him: enormously tall, craggy and grey like the rocks around us. Grey hair, grey clothes, grey skin.

It was wonderful to see him again. I knew that whatever was going on, Keeper would help make it right.

"But I am no longer Keeper," he said. "I have a new name."

Maddy looked shocked. "Why?"

"I made the nexus ring. When we learned how dangerous it was, I kept it safe, so I was Keeper, although I did not do that very well. Then I destroyed it, so now I am Destroyer."

Maddy leaned against him for a moment. "Destroyer is such a scary name. Can't you be something else?" She stared into space for a moment. "How about Ring

Crusher?" she asked, her eyes lit up and her face eager.

Keeper laughed, in great bellows that echoed off the mountains. The magic folk all turned to us. He called out, "The children do not like my new name. They think I should be called Ring Crusher."

The crowd roared with laughter. Keeper laughed so hard tears ran down his face.

"Why is that so funny?" Maddy asked, looking offended.

He patted her shoulder, knocking her over. He caught her and stood her up again. "Ring Crusher is not a name for a grown giant." He laughed again.

"Why not?" I asked, checking that Maddy wasn't hurt.

"That is a baby name, for baby giants – a sweet, funny name. 'Oh, look at little Ring Crusher.' That is not a name for a fully grown giant. And sometimes giant names change." He smiled and patted her again, very gently this time.

Like Maddy, I hated the name Destroyer. I wasn't about to stop calling him Keeper. "Why did you send for us?" I asked.

"The tears in the veil will not heal. We have tried everything we know, and have failed. Now we need you, my magic boy."

I shook my head. "I have no idea what to do."

"We will help you figure it out."

I wanted to argue, but Maddy slipped her hand into

Keeper's huge one, and asked, "Are Gatherings always here?"

"Oh no," said Keeper. "A Gathering will be wherever it is needed. But always in a place comfortable for all magic folk. We need meadow and forest, sky and cliffs and water. All are safe at a Gathering."

I wondered about that as I watched the crows tease a pack of wolves. They flew just out of reach, cawing and scolding. The wolves would lie very still, until a crow flew too close. Then a wolf would lunge and the crow would fly off in a squawking, feather-flying scramble. But soon they were at it again.

"Corvus, the crows should leave the wolves alone," I yelled.

"We can handle them ourselves," a large grey wolf growled.

That's what worries me, I thought. I gestured for the crows to join us, and to be quiet. "Who comes to a Gathering?" I asked.

"Only the locals," said Keeper.

"What do you mean?" Maddy asked.

He smiled down at her. "Well, there are no mermaids, no ocean spirits."

"But other spirits?" I asked.

"Yes. There are tree spirits and water spirits and mountain spirits." He pointed to Castle Mountain, looming above us.

I could see something moving on the mountain,

like mist shifting and reforming, sometimes dark, sometimes shining.

"That is the spirit of Storm Mountain," he said.

"Shouldn't a mountain spirit be big and solid, like you?" Maddy asked.

"Oh, no," said Keeper. He thought for a moment, struggling to explain. "Do you feel like this," and he gestured to himself, "when you look at a mountain? Big and slow? Of course not. Your spirit soars, like an eagle. That is why eagles like mountains – they dance with the mountain spirits."

I became quiet, letting magic fill me, and I began to feel the spirits all around – in the trees, in the air, on the mountainside. They were intriguing but eerie, and I decided I was glad they weren't usually so noticeable.

"The glaciers did not come," said Keeper, his voice sombre.

"What?" I asked.

"Glacier spirits feel too threatened, more than any of us. They do not like to travel far." He sighed. "They used to be great travellers." Keeper looked sad for a moment, and then shook his head as the crows began teasing the wolves again.

When I started to call them off, Keeper said, "They will be fine. Once a Gathering is called, none can harm any magic folk arriving, at the Gathering, or departing." I could hear a resonance in his words as if the magic world agreed, as if his words literally rang true. It felt like old magic.

"Not even Gronvald?" Maddy asked, glancing around and looking nervous.

"No, not even Gronvald. Although he never comes. He would be welcome if he did. A Gathering is for all magic folk."

Keeper guided us to the side of the Gathering, near the buffalo. Then he walked towards a large rock, a centre point for the crowd. As the magic folk noticed, they turned towards him and slowly became quiet.

Maddy poked me. "Josh, the buffalo are singing!"

I turned with a laugh, to tell her not to be silly, when I heard the song:

> *Buffalo gals, won't you come out tonight,*
> *come out tonight, come out tonight?*
> *Buffalo gals, won't you come out tonight,*
> *and dance by the light of the moon.*

The smaller buffalo sang softly, her voice low and rumbly.

The other buffalo stepped closer and said, "Dear one, the Gathering is about to begin."

The singing buffalo stopped, and they stood still, huge heads together, facing the centre of the Gathering.

Maddy and I stared at each other. We'd seen a lot of strange things in the magic world, but this...this was just weird. We started to laugh, and then struggled to be quiet. We leaned against each other, shoulders shaking.

Keeper cleared his throat in an *eh-hem* that shook the ground, and everyone became silent.

He cleared his throat again, a little more softly. "We, the magic folk of this place, have come together for a Gathering. We are only of this place, but we must act for the entire magic world. This weight is upon us."

As he spoke, it was as if this was another magical invocation. I felt the importance of the decision to be made descend on us all.

Keeper continued. "The nexus ring has torn the veil. This has happened before, but now the tears are not healing. The nexus ring has been destroyed, but we have not found a way to repair the veil." He pointed at the doorway. "Magic is leaking into the human world."

All the magic folk stared at the tear, as if together they should have enough magic to repair it.

The larger buffalo snorted. "I cannot see a thing," he said. "I never did get the hang of seeing magic."

Maddy walked to his side and held out her ring. "Look through this," she said.

He peered through the tiny ring and gasped. "Ah. This is a wondrous ring, indeed! Look, my dear!"

The other buffalo leaned in and squinted through the ring. "Oh, my. This is terrible!" She shook her head and woofed softly.

The first buffalo said, in a firm voice, "Something

needs to be done!" But he didn't offer any ideas.

Keeper had continued talking. I tuned in to hear him say, "Not only the otter-people are suffering. All magic folk are suffering, and we will suffer more as more magic leaks out. It must be stopped."

Keeper looked around, spotted me, and gestured for me to join him. I closed my eyes and groaned. I had to stand in the centre of them all?

Maddy slipped in beside me and held my hand.

"Maddy, you're not in this," I said.

"Of course I am."

I would never have guessed how much strength I could draw from holding her small hand.

As Maddy and I joined him, Keeper continued. "This human boy, Josh, has magical strengths that grow beyond anything we have seen. We ask the Gathering to support him in trying to repair the veil."

The magic folk were silent. I wondered if they were simply shocked at the absurdity of what Keeper proposed.

Then a bear stood on its hind legs and growled out a long phrase. Keeper translated. "A human boy cannot do this. He is too weak."

A porcupine added, "He cannot feed himself. He must warm himself with *fire*. He could not survive one night without help."

"I could understand the porcupine," whispered Maddy, "but not the bear."

Softly, Keeper said, "Some animals can manage human languages better than others."

A moose called out, a strained, creaky sound. Keeper translated. "Our weak ones drown."

"Or we eat them," said a wolf, her teeth gleaming.

"A human boy could not possibly have the magic we need," roared a voice from deep in the crowd. It sounded like another giant.

Maddy growled and held up her ring. "If you can't see his magic, you are welcome to look through my elven ring."

No one took up her offer. They all stared at me. I could feel magic radiating from me and I knew they could see it too.

Then Aleena stood. Her black cloak swirled behind her as she walked, swaying like she was moving under water. Staying away from Keeper, she gently moved Maddy back so she could stand at my side.

"He is just a boy, you say, and yet he kept the nexus ring from me, and he kept it from Gronvald. He can cross the veil without tiring. He can use firestone. He can water travel. He has travelled deep into the earth. There are some here who can do some of these things, but not one of us can do all of them. Not one of us has the power this boy has, and he is just beginning."

Arguments broke out all across the meadow, in a chaos of noise.

Then Greyfur staggered up, still weak and pale.

"*Ssst!* This talk is useless." He had an intensity that filled the valley, and the magic folk honoured it with their silence. "This boy, this *human* boy," (there was that scorn again, in the way he said human), "can do what no human should be able to do. *Tss.* He can touch our magic. He can use our magic."

The crowd hissed.

"That makes him magic folk."

More hisses, and a cry, "But he's *human!*"

"Yes, human and magic. *Tss.* We have not had one before. We have had humans live in our world in happiness, *hnn*, like Maddy, but none who were strong in magic. Only this boy."

The crowd booed and hissed.

Greyfur held up a hand for silence and continued. "Veil was created by Ancients Ones. There are no Ancient Ones now. Only veil and tears. *Ssst!* And this boy. Only this boy has hope of fixing tears."

I choked on that.

"Only this boy, this magic human boy, can repair veil between human and magic worlds."

But how? my brain was screaming. No one else seemed to care about that. They listened and thought and then the larger buffalo spoke. "Let the boy do it. The boy will fix the veil." And they believed it, like the problem was already solved. They yelped and howled and cawed; I just felt incredulous. What did they think I was going to do?

Keeper raised a huge hand and the magic folk grew silent again. He called out, "Is it the Will of the Gathering to support Josh in his effort to repair the veil?"

The magic folk shouted their approval, the birds cawing and trilling, gruff *hurrahs* from the buffalo. I heard some grumbles, but once it was clear that most magic folk approved, the grumbling stopped.

"Then this is the Decision of the Gathering, and all are bound by it." Keeper's voice resonated with power again, with the old magic of the Gathering.

"What does that mean?" I asked Keeper, as he turned to Maddy and me.

"It means we all must help you, whatever you need, so use it carefully."

I felt burdened by this task, by their trust and support. They would give me anything I asked? That was too much! This was all too much. But when I turned to tell them, everyone was leaving. The Gathering was over.

CHAPTER FOUR

THE ANCIENT ONES

I STOOD STARING AS CREATURES LEFT — RUNNING, flying, or simply vanishing into the forest. Aleena walked to the lakeshore, ready to water travel, to become water and flow as water, but Keeper called out to her. "Aleena, we may need your help."

She stood, one foot in the lake, looking like she'd rather be anywhere else. But something in Keeper's face held her. She closed her eyes for a moment, nodded and stepped back from the water's edge.

When the buffalo walked past, the larger one said, "If there's any way we can help, let us know."

"Thank you," said Keeper.

As they walked down the shore of the lake, I could hear a low, rumbly song drifting back on the breeze:

Land of the silver birch,
home of the beaver...

"There are buffalo in the magic world?" asked Maddy.

"Of course," said Keeper. "There always were. Then, when the buffalo in the human world were being hunted and we realized humans were going to kill them all, we opened doorways and rescued whole herds. Some have absorbed more magic than others." He nodded at the buffalo walking down the valley. "They came from the human world. As they soaked up magic, they found their voices. They love to talk and sing."

Maddy giggled. I thought it was oddly sweet and a little comforting that something human wasn't despised.

We joined Greyfur and Eneirda beside the lake. Aleena sat on the opposite side of the group from Keeper. The crows joined us, Corvus strutting on the ground beside me, the others perched or flying nearby. The little girl crow leaned against my knee.

"Beloved of crows," Maddy muttered.

"Shush," I said. But I gently petted the crow's soft back.

When we were all settled, Maddy said, "No one else is going to help?"

"We called the Gathering," said Keeper, nodding to Greyfur, Eneirda and Corvus. "Now we know the Will of the Gathering. The others will help if we ask. That is enough."

"Now it is up to Josh," said Eneirda.

"I don't know what to do," I said. "How can I fix the veil?"

"*Tss*. If you cannot, we all will die," said Greyfur.

"You must find a way," said Keeper.

Corvus cawed in agreement.

But how? I borrowed Maddy's ring and walked over to the doorway. Through the ring, I could see a gold line marking its edge, and a gash stretching across it. Magic poured out, golden as honey. All around the tear, magic was pale and thin, as if it had been drained off.

I touched the edge of the veil and hung on as magic poured up my arm. I could feel the veil stretching around the world, woven of threads as fine as spider's silk. I could feel the tears in all the doorways the nexus ring had been through, and feel magic flowing into the human world.

I grabbed both sides of the veil and pulled them together. They touched and light flared, but I couldn't get the edges to connect. Frustrated, I muttered, "To fix something, you need the right tools, like a needle and thread to sew up a hole. I don't know what I need, or if it's even possible to repair it."

"You'll find a way. We'll all help you," Maddy said, nodding towards the group beside the lake. Then her eyes widened. "Maybe breakfast will help!"

She had a huge grin on her face as she checked out the meal Keeper and the otter-people set out for us. Keeper had lit a fire – he was heating water for mint tea and grilling meat. Buns were lined up at the edge of the fire, warming. A small bowl full of dried berries sat nearby.

"You have buns?" Maddy asked.

Keeper nodded. "Usually I bake my own but these are a gift from a park warden, a friend of mine."

When I looked surprised, Keeper laughed. "I have many friends."

Starving, we settled in to feast. Once I was full, I sat back and started to think again. "How was the veil created?" I asked.

"Aleena is the best storyteller," said Keeper. I could hear disapproval in his voice, as he remembered the trouble she'd created before she understood the damage caused by the nexus ring.

I could tell that Aleena heard it too; her pale skin grew even more pale and her eyes darkened and snapped in anger. But she stayed – perhaps the Will of the Gathering held her.

"Long ago," she said, "the Ancient Ones helped the earth grow. They taught living things magic, and embedded it in the rocks, in water and ice, in the very air we breathe. They drew it from sunlight and moonlight and stardust."

Aleena spoke in her beautiful voice like she was

weaving a story. She was a natural storyteller, her voice soft and fluid. She was beautiful to watch, too, if you didn't know how scary she could be.

"They worked to keep magic in the world, as humans multiplied and learned to build. Some humans remembered magic, but more forgot, enamoured with building, making and doing. Eventually the Ancient Ones gave up on humans and divided the world in two – one for magic and one for humans – and set the veil between."

Eneirda nodded her approval.

"Where are they now?" I asked.

"They are no more," said Aleena.

"What happened to them?" asked Maddy.

Greyfur answered. "No one knows, *hnn*. When the veil was, they were not."

"But what *happened* to them?" Maddy asked again, sounding stubborn.

Keeper shrugged.

"Maddy, come with me," I said.

She followed me back to the doorway.

"Hold up your ring."

She slipped her ring off her finger and held it up for me to peer through.

Watching through the ring, I grabbed both sides of the tear, hung on past the initial shock of magic, and settled into the veil. I could feel every gash. When I settled deeper I could feel time moving along the veil. I went even deeper, until I could hear the veil singing. I knew I was hearing the song of the Ancient Ones. But I still had no idea how to fix the tears.

Maddy and I walked back to the shore of the lake. "I need to know what happened to the Ancient Ones," I announced. "I must know more about them." I'd been expecting arguments, but when I said *must*, magic came with it, insisting.

"I don't know any more about them," said Aleena.

"Nor do I," said Keeper. "There are few who would know such old stories."

"None of us know," said Greyfur.

Corvus cawed, and Keeper interpreted. "Giants are not old enough. The spirits are too old – their time sense is too large. They cannot focus on little details like this."

"So who is older than the giants, but not as old as the spirits?" I asked.

Everyone looked uncomfortable as the Will of the Gathering pressed upon them.

"Gronvald is not old enough," said Aleena, uneasy at even mentioning his name. "But he has a long memory, especially for anyone who harms him. He hates the veil – it slows him down. So he hates the Ancient Ones."

Keeper nodded. "Trolls know many stories. They pass on knowledge of caves and metal and jewels. They remember every detail."

"So, what do we do?" I asked. "Just go visit him?" I shuddered.

Maddy said, "Let's go for tea. I'm sure he'll be overjoyed to see us." She laughed, but it sounded a little hysterical.

"He will not want to see us. But he will, if it is the Will of the Gathering."

"I need to talk to him," I said.

Keeper and Corvus conferred – it looked like they were arguing. Finally Keeper repeated, "It is the Will of the Gathering."

Corvus squawked in response. He cawed to two crows and they flew to Keeper's cave. Then Corvus chose two others, and left with them.

I was getting frustrated with not being able to understand crow. I could feel his disagreement, but not catch the words. Maddy and I looked at Keeper, waiting for an explanation.

"Corvus and his friends have gone to inform Gronvald that it is the Will of the Gathering that he speak with us."

But I really don't want to talk to him, I thought. Maddy slipped her hand into mine. I glanced down – had she become a mind reader?

"Will they be safe?" asked Maddy. "What if Gronvald hurts them?"

"They fly at the Will of the Gathering," said Keeper. "He will not harm them." Then he smiled. "Although he will do everything he can to scare them!"

"And the others?" Maddy asked, pointing towards Keeper's cave.

Keeper watched for a few moments, and nodded as the birds flew out of his cave, carrying something between them.

"They bring gold for Gronvald," said Keeper. "His fee. He will not want to speak to us, even with the Will of the Gathering requiring that he help us. The gold will make it easier for him."

The crows dropped the bag at Keeper's feet. The small canvas sack clanked as it fell. Keeper untied it so we could see in – it was filled with shining gold coins.

"So he'll help us?" Maddy asked.

"No. He will not want to tell us anything," said Keeper, smiling.

"Then why are we going?" I asked, still hoping to avoid Gronvald.

"He will not want us to repair the veil. The tears make it easier for him to travel to the human world to steal gold. But he will talk to us. We may be able to learn something useful from him."

Keeper stood and dropped the bag of coins into a huge jacket pocket. When Greyfur and Eneirda moved to join us, Keeper shook his head. "No, you must rest. You have done enough. Aleena will come with us."

Greyfur, Eneirda and Aleena all looked horrified. Each one of them wanted to argue, clearly hating

Keeper's decision, but they didn't say a thing. They looked to me, hoping I would offer a different Will of the Gathering, but I shook my head. I had to trust Keeper.

Keeper led Maddy, Aleena and me up beyond the head of the lake. "We will walk to Gronvald's nearest cave," said Keeper.

"His *nearest* cave?" Maddy asked, skipping to keep up with Keeper. He slowed and held out a hand. She grabbed one finger and they walked together.

I followed, the crows circling me, Aleena trailing behind.

"Gronvald does not like to carry treasure too far, after he has stolen it. So he has many caves."

"Don't other people – um, magic folk, like trolls – steal from his caves when he's not there?" Maddy asked.

"Gronvald is very good with guarding magic. None can pass if he does not wish it."

"Why does the Will of the Gathering affect Gronvald? He wasn't there."

"That does not matter. It is binding on all magic folk."

"Like a law?"

"Do humans sometimes choose to disobey a law?" Keeper asked.

"Well, sure. Some do."

"We cannot choose to disregard the Will of the Gathering. We may not like it, and we may not be generous about it, but we must cooperate. This is very old magic."

"What if the Will of the Gathering was to do something really wrong, really harmful?" Maddy asked.

"Why would we agree to that?" asked Keeper. Then he said in a gentle voice, "We are not humans, Maddy."

We hiked up the valley along the creek that fed the lake below us. As we turned to follow a smaller creek, Corvus joined us. He cawed and Keeper nodded. "He will be waiting for us?"

Corvus squawked once, and then we all headed up the mountain. When I grew too nervous about meeting Gronvald, I distracted myself by sketching in the air with one finger, just quick sketches of the mountain ridges.

We left the creek where it cut deep into the rocks in a narrow gorge, and hiked across the face of the mountain, quickly moving above the treeline.

Keeper lifted Maddy onto his shoulder and took my hand to help me climb the slope. The crows flew high above, and Aleena panted quietly behind us. We followed the curve of the mountain to the north side, cold and bright with snow.

Finally, we reached an opening in the cliff face. Keeper held out the bag of coins and shook it. Clinking echoed in the cave.

Maybe he won't be here, I thought, feeling desperate. *Maybe that noise from the back of the cave is a bear that Keeper can scare off. Maybe...*

And then Gronvald stood in the entrance to his cave, glowering.

He had the perfect face for glowering. His eyes were small and dark, his eyebrows darker. He was short and thick and lumpy, with ears that stuck out and a nose that reminded me of the stem of our pumpkin.

"Welcome," he said, sneering at us. Only Keeper wasn't afraid.

"We need to speak with you," said Keeper. He held out the bag of gold and shook it again.

Gronvald nodded and bowed his head a little, to welcome us into his cave. Keeper ducked his head and walked in.

Looking pale, Aleena said, "I'll wait out here," and slipped away.

The crows surrounded Maddy and me as we entered the cave. Gronvald roared at them, flapping his arms and bellowing. They scattered, scrambling out of the cave, except for Corvus. He stood his ground, wings spread wide, cawing. Muttering curses, Gronvald let him stay.

The cave was dark, with torchlight shining off piles of rocks glinting with gold. Wooden boxes of ore were stacked along the walls. More piles gleamed beyond us, deep in the cave. Coins in piles and small sacks like Keeper's filled the gaps. It smelled musty and rank. Small bones littered the ground.

Maddy was quivering, scared of the dark and the

bones and Gronvald. I turned to her, and put my face right into a spider's web. I yelped, clawing at my face, desperate to pull it off. Gronvald smirked. Maddy stifled a laugh and helped me. Pulling the threads out of my hair, I could see a fly wrapped in a cocoon, waiting to be eaten.

As I shook off the last strands, the spider was flung across the room, straight at Gronvald. With a shriek he threw up his hands and leapt back. For a moment he looked embarrassed, and then just mad.

Keeper hid a smile and settled himself on the floor of the cave, leaning against the wall. Corvus landed on a box of gold ore and began to peck at the rocks. Maddy and I sat beside him. I picked up a chunk of rock – I could see pockets of gold, bright in the darker rock. I ran my finger over a vein of gold and thought about the ways gold was used in art.

"Do Not Touch My GOLD!" roared Gronvald.

I looked up to see him charging at me, furious. I stood and staggered sideways. "You can't hurt me. I'm here at the Will of the Gathering," I choked out.

He didn't stop, didn't slow, just shifted the direction of his lunge and grabbed Maddy, his hands closing around her neck. I flung myself at his back, but I couldn't budge him.

Corvus flew into Gronvald's face, flapping and pecking. Gronvald took one hand off Maddy to fling him away, smacking him into the cave wall. Maddy sucked in a huge breath, and then both of Gronvald's hands were around her neck again. I pounded on his back and twisted his ears, but he shook me off.

Keeper lunged, grabbed Gronvald's shirt at the back of his neck and simply lifted him. Gronvald's hands dropped from Maddy as he tried to beat off Keeper, but Keeper ignored him, lifting him until they were nose to nose.

"STOP!" he bellowed.

Gronvald shuddered and stopped, even though his face was twisted in rage.

I stood, holding Maddy while she panted, still fighting to breathe. "Thanks," I said to Corvus. When he nodded and cawed I knew exactly what he meant. *You are our magic boy.*

Keeper gave Gronvald a shake, and then set him down.

"Get out. GET OUT!" Gronvald growled, furious.

Keeper simply pulled out the bag and poured gold coins into his huge, cupped hand. When Gronvald reached for them, Keeper closed his hand over the pile. I could see Gronvald's longing, almost as if it had its own magic, driving him to hoard gold.

Gronvald hissed in frustration. "Get on with it, then. That won't buy you much time. And don't touch my gold," he snapped at Corvus, who'd straightened his ruffled feathers and was pecking at the gold again.

Keeper nodded to me.

I cleared my throat. "What can you tell us about the

Ancient Ones?"

Gronvald didn't even look at me. He stared at Keeper, and said, "*You* have purchased my time. Only you."

Keeper growled, low in his throat, and said, "Fine. What can you tell me about the Ancient Ones?"

Gronvald glanced at Maddy, Corvus and me, and frowned.

"They are here as my assistants," Keeper said. "They will only listen."

Gronvald nodded. "I never met the Ancient Ones."

"Of course you did not. What do you know about them?"

"Only what the stories tell."

"Which is?" When Gronvald paused, Keeper poured the coins back into the bag.

Gronvald snarled. "They made the veil. They are no more." He smiled at me, but I knew he wasn't really smiling. His eyes were threatening, saying very clearly, *I like the tears in the veil. Leave them alone if you want me to leave you alone.*

Shivering, I thought, *Fine with me.* But I couldn't leave. Even though the Will of the Gathering didn't bind me, I felt driven to help.

"We have to fix the tears!" Maddy burst out. "Magic is leaking out of your world. It's harming *your world!*"

Gronvald grimaced, turned away from Maddy, and spoke to Keeper. "I do not believe humans. I do not listen to humans. I do not speak to humans."

"We're trying to help," I snapped.

Gronvald spat at me. "You expect me to believe that anything a *human* could do would be good for the magic world?" His voice shook with anger.

When Maddy opened her mouth to argue, Keeper held up a hand to stop her. "What else do you know about the Ancient Ones?"

"Nothing. The Ancient Ones are gone, long gone. They put so much of themselves into the veil, they lost all their power. They only had a little weaving magic left." Then he snapped his mouth shut, looking uncomfortable.

"Weaving magic?" I asked. "What's that?"

He ignored me.

Keeper studied him, thinking. Finally he said, "Tell me about weaving magic."

Gronvald stared back, pondering. We waited, and waited a little more, and then Gronvald spoke. "Your time is up." He grinned and held out his hand. As soon as Keeper tossed him the bag, he opened it and poured the gold into his lap, counting and caressing the coins.

As we left, I glanced back. Gronvald was watching with narrowed eyes, tightly focused on me.

CHAPTER FIVE

BROX AND VIVIENNE

W E WERE ALL RELIEVED TO BE AWAY from Gronvald. Even the deep shade on the north face of the mountain was better than the oppressive darkness of the cave. But it was still cold. Maddy and I shoved our hands into our pockets and walked faster, trying to get warm. Keeper walked with us. Aleena trailed behind again. The crows rose in a flock, squawking and scolding, making their dislike of Gronvald clear.

I thought about weaving as we hiked. I'd seen a demonstration once – the weaver working at a loom, throwing a shuttle loaded with thread back and forth over lines of thread held tight on the frame. Then I thought about spiders' webs, trying to focus on how the web was woven, not how it felt sticking to my face.

Maddy picked up some fluff from a seed head and started teasing it apart with her fingers. "Josh, could the veil really be woven?" she asked.

"It looks woven," I said, "of the finest threads imaginable. Like spider's silk," I added, "but not so sticky."

She grinned. "If we found someone who could weave, could they fix it?"

"I don't know how, unless they have some connection to the Ancient Ones. Do any magic folk weave?" I asked Keeper.

"A little simple weaving," he said.

"Fine weaving?"

Corvus cawed.

"Yes," said Aleena to Corvus, reluctantly. "There are the weavers."

"Who are they?" I asked.

"I don't really know," she said. "They stay to themselves – they don't like visitors."

"But can they weave?" I could feel the Will of the Gathering insisting on answers.

"Oh, yes. They can weave anything. But..."

"But what?" asked Maddy.

"They don't like visitors. They really don't like visitors. They have a guardian..." She swallowed.

"Then we'll get past him," I said.

"But –"

"We have to talk to them. Can you take us there?"

"I'm not sure exactly where they are."

Corvus spoke again, in a long string of caws and squawks and muttering. Keeper and Aleena listened intently. I couldn't understand anything he said.

When he was finished, Keeper nodded. "Up the Rockwall," he said, without explaining. "It is too far for you to walk."

Aleena sighed. "I could take them."

"Water travel? You could keep them warm while you're travelling, but how would you dry them, up there in November?" Keeper asked.

Aleena looked us over and frowned, as if she'd forgotten we were humans.

"We could go by boat with otter-people," Maddy said. "Not Greyfur and Eneirda – they're too tired. But someone else?"

Keeper shook his head. "The Bow River was risk enough in winter."

I shivered, remembering.

"This route is higher and colder, in a smaller river, with a storm coming. It would not be safe for you." Keeper paused to think, and then said, "You can travel with Brox and Vivienne."

"Brox and Vivienne," Aleena scoffed. "Stupid, smelly and clumsy!"

Keeper growled his disapproval.

"Who are they?" I asked.

"They are the buffalo who were at the Gathering."

"We're going to travel by buffalo?" said Maddy,

sounding nervous and excited at the same time.

I didn't care how I got there, as long as I could learn more about the veil.

Keeper said, "Corvus, could you ask them to return to the lake?"

Corvus cawed and flew off, towards the lake far below us. We followed more slowly, enjoying the warmth of the sun on our faces.

When we reached the lake, Aleena said goodbye and walked to the shore.

Keeper stopped her with a hand held high. "Aleena, I have a task for you."

She waited, one foot in the water. "I need to leave now," she said, her face tight.

I knew how much she hated Gronvald and feared Keeper, and how much she wanted to be far from them.

"It is the Will of the Gathering," said Keeper.

"*You* are not the Will of the Gathering," she said. "Only Josh."

Keeper turned to me. "I do not trust Gronvald. He will do whatever he can to stop you, to work around the Will of the Gathering. I would like Aleena to follow him."

Aleena gasped and stepped backwards into the lake. "No! The crows can do it."

The crows cawed agreement, but Keeper shook his head. "The crows cannot follow Gronvald through his caves."

"Neither can I," said Aleena, panic in her voice.

"But you can follow his scent in water. You can alert the crows when he comes above ground."

"I won't do it," she said.

She looked afraid, but fierce too, and powerful. I felt totally intimidated. I closed my eyes for a moment, and then I spoke. "Aleena, you and Maddy and I caused many of the tears in the veil. I helped you escape from deep in the earth. Now you must do this."

I could see when the magic of the Will of the Gathering reached her. I could see her battle it, her eyes darkening, her face tight and pale. Then she accepted it. With a slightly bowed head and a flat voice, she said, "I will follow him."

"Thank you." I knew what this was costing her, the fear she was fighting.

She nodded stiffly. "I will contact the crows when I have news." Then she dove into the lake and vanished.

Maddy and I hiked up Castle Mountain with Keeper. His cave was cozy and welcoming. A huge bed filled one corner, piled high with striped wool blankets. A collection of odd-sized chairs gathered around a wooden slab table, and shelves lined the walls.

Keeper walked straight to the massive stone fireplace on one wall of the cave, added firewood, and knelt to blow on the coals. Flames leapt up, warming and lighting the cave.

A large iron pot sat near the fire; he lifted it and

hung it above the flames. Then he lined up enormous buns on the hearth. "They will warm here," he said.

Soon the smell of stew and buns filled the cave. I could hear Maddy's stomach growling.

Slowly we peeled off layers of hats and mitts and jackets as we roasted ourselves by the fire. By the time we were thoroughly warm, the stew was bubbling. Keeper ladled some into a huge wooden bowl for himself, and into his two smallest bowls for Maddy and me.

"Half full is plenty," I said, eyeing what to us would be serving dishes.

"You are not hungry?" he asked, ladle hovering over a bowl.

"Starving," said Maddy. "And half full is lots."

We ate our stew with large wooden spoons, sipping off the sides. We each ate a bun, even though they were the size of small loaves of bread. Then we went back for more stew. When we were finished, Keeper filled buns with thick slices of meat, and wrapped them in an almost clean cloth for our next meal.

While we roasted and rested and felt too full by the fire, Keeper headed into his back caves. We could hear him rummaging around, cursing occasionally when he thought we couldn't hear him. He returned with his arms overflowing. He dumped everything on the table and started sorting.

"Josh, Maddy, help me here," he said. He pulled out two sets of leather bags. The first he hung on me, one pouch in front and one in back. "Brox and Vivienne will carry your bags while you are with them. But you will need to carry them sometimes, too." He pulled on the leather straps, tugging them shorter and shorter, until the pouches hung against my chest and back, instead of banging my knees. When he was satisfied, he started on Maddy's. He had to punch new holes in the straps to make them short enough, but eventually, he was satisfied with hers, too.

He gave us each a leather sack of water, although he told us we would be near water for most of our journey. Then he packed the bags with food, including the buns he'd wrapped for us earlier.

"Do you have a firestone?" he asked.

"Yes," I said, slipping it out of my pocket to show him.

"And you have your ring?" he asked Maddy.

She held it up.

"Brox and Vivienne will take care of you. Corvus will travel with you. You will spend the night with otter-people. The Will of the Gathering requires all must help you with whatever you ask." Then he paused.

"Josh, Maddy." He shook his head, and cleared his throat. "We ask a great deal of you. I wish..." He paused again. "I created the nexus ring. I did not keep it safe, and I cannot fix the veil. That falls to you, and it should not. I am sorry." He sighed.

"I would come if I could, but it is too far for you to

walk. I am too large to ride a buffalo, and too slow to keep up with them. I am confident you will find a way. You have a deep magic, Josh. And Maddy will help you."

She nodded, looking determined.

We wrapped ourselves in all our layers. Maddy wasn't sure about putting her fur hat back on.

I grinned and pulled out her red hat. Her eyes lit up when she saw it. As she tugged it down over her ears, she said, "Thanks. It feels terrible wearing fur around furry friends."

With her purple jacket and the red hat, flaps over her ears and strings dangling, she looked ready for a party. I was more sombre, in black and grey. It suited how I felt, needing to protect the magic world without knowing how to do it. We slipped on the leather bags, even though Keeper offered to carry them, and headed down the mountain. Keeper's arms were full again, wrapped around bundles of fur.

Crows flew with us as we followed the shore of the lake. I could feel their anxiety, their need to keep moving.

The little girl crow settled on my shoulder again, murmuring softly. I ran a finger down her back. "What's your name?" I said.

She cawed back like she was answering me.

I tried to copy her and failed miserably. I swear she laughed at me.

I laughed back. "I'll just have to call you Crow Baby."

"Crowby," she muttered. "Crowby."

I smiled and patted her again. "You speak English much better than I speak crow. Crowby it is."

We met the buffalo near the stream that drained the lake. Now that we had to ride them, they looked scary and huge, as they snuffled and snorted and shook their massive heads.

"Brox, Vivienne," said Keeper, nodding to each of them. "Thank you for returning. We need you to help Josh and Maddy."

They stared at Maddy and me. "Us?" the larger buffalo said, sounding puzzled. "You want us to work with humans?"

Brox, I thought. *This one is Brox.*

"They are trying to help," said Vivienne, the smaller buffalo.

"Yes, then I suppose we should help them," said Brox. "And it is the Will of the Gathering." He sighed, in a great snuffly wheeze. "Very well."

"They would like to meet the weavers," said Keeper.

"Ah, the weavers," said Brox, nodding ponderously.

"Hmmm," said Vivienne. It sounded almost like a hum.

Then they looked at Keeper and waited.

"Oh," said Keeper, realizing he needed to say more. "Uh, could you take them?"

"*Take* them?" said Brox. "To the weavers? Ah...yes... well...that would be interesting, wouldn't it, Vivienne?"

But he didn't say it like going to a party might be interesting. It sounded more like he would be curious to see how it turned out.

"You know the way?" asked Keeper.

Brox looked offended. "Of course we do. Buffalo are great travellers."

Keeper nodded. "Take Josh and Maddy to the otter-people beyond Storm Mountain for the night. They will help – it is the Will of the Gathering."

Then he looked at what we'd carried down from his cave. "Well, then – let me get you organized," he said, a little gruffly. He took our leather bags and reset the buckles to make the straps as long as possible. He made sure Maddy and I saw exactly what he was doing, and that we could reset them ourselves. "Because buffalo cannot work with buckles."

No kidding, I thought.

We both stared at the buffalo while Keeper settled the leather bags on their huge backs. He slung mine on Brox, shifting it back and forth until Brox was comfortable. Then he lifted Maddy's onto Vivienne's slightly less huge back.

The buffalo were tall, broader than horses and covered in coarse, thick fur. They had big shaggy heads, with wicked-looking curving horns and large hard noses.

"Have you never seen a buffalo?" asked Brox, when he caught us staring.

"There aren't any more – well, only in a few places.

But I've never seen..." I stammered.

Maddy said, "Only, well, heads on walls, and furs. Sorry."

I turned to her, shocked. "Maddy, don't say that," I whispered. "That's worse than wearing a fur hat!"

Brox harrumphed. "It is the truth of what humans did."

"These children did not kill any buffalo," said Vivienne.

Ignoring them, Keeper lifted Maddy onto Vivienne's back, settled her, and turned to me.

"I can get up myself," I said, but when I stood beside Brox, I realized I had no hope of reaching.

Keeper laughed as he lifted me. "You will need to use a fallen tree or a large rock to climb up and down. Always help Maddy – it is a longer fall for her."

I wiggled while he held me, trying to get comfortable sitting on such a broad back. That's when the smell hit me: strong, musky, with a sharp tang. I tried not to breathe too deeply. But the fur was lovely. The outer hairs were coarse but under them was a thick layer of fine, soft fur. I wiggled my fingers into it, enjoying the softness and the warmth.

Keeper shook out a bundle he'd carried down from his cave, a large fur blanket. He tucked it around Maddy, fur side down, anchoring it under her legs. Then he brought one to me, tucking me in just as snuggly.

What was it? I wondered. What kind of fur would be okay to use around furred creatures? I flipped up an edge – it was buffalo.

"Keeper," I said, shocked. "We can't ride buffalo wrapped in buffalo hides!"

Keeper cleared his throat. "Animals die. I use what is left, after."

Brox blew through his nostrils. "They would be honoured to be of use, to be of benefit even after their deaths."

Maddy and I glanced at each other, both of us confused by buffalo logic.

"Are you all set?" Keeper asked.

"I don't even know where we're going," I said.

Keeper nodded. "Brox and Vivienne know the way. And they will bring you back to me, here." He turned to Brox. "Send a crow when it is time to meet."

Brox nodded, and the crows cawed in agreement. Snorting loudly, Brox turned onto the path down the mountain, and Vivienne followed.

"Goodbye," Maddy and I called to Keeper.

He smiled and waved.

As we headed down the mountain, Vivienne began to sing:

Oh, give me a home where the buffalo roam,
where the deer and the antelope play,
where seldom is heard a discouraging word,

and the sky is not cloudy all day.

When I looked back at Keeper, he was still watching, his face serious.

CHAPTER SIX

BUFFALO TRAVEL

THE NEXT TWO DAYS WERE A MISERY. Total, complete misery. Our legs were rubbed raw and our spines jolted into agony. Uphill was bad. Downhill was worse. Maddy and I were desperate to walk, but Brox wouldn't let us.

"Keeper asked us to take you to the weavers. We will do as he asked. If he thought you could walk, he would be walking with you. But we are faster."

They were faster. The magic did something to them, making them really good travellers. They always knew where they were, always knew where to go next, always knew the best path. We covered ground faster than any horse could, and squeezed down paths I would have thought were much too narrow.

As fast as we travelled, though, it was never fast

enough for the crows. They were always pushing, always urging us on. Soon I was feeling it too, an anxiety to do something, to accomplish something, to fix this.

While we travelled, Brox talked, except when Vivienne chose to sing.

"Why do you like human songs so much?" Maddy asked.

Vivienne shook her head. "Not human songs. All songs. I like to sing. If otter-people had songs, I'd sing those, too."

I laughed, imagining Eneirda's look of horror if she heard this.

"I tried bird songs..." She shook her head again and woofed softly.

"We like to slip into the human world and listen by campfires," said Brox. "That's where Vivienne learns her songs. And I learn a great deal, too." He rumbled at the back of his throat, and continued.

"We're heading southwest, from Castle across the Bow Valley," Brox said. "I'm using human names so it will make sense to you. We'll climb over the ridge towards Storm Mountain, down into the valley, and keep heading southwest to the Rockwall. It's all in a straight line – rather surprising, really, for mountain travel. We usually only see that in the prairies. Of course, there's lots of up and down to make it interesting."

I groaned. Interesting wasn't what I would call it.

By late afternoon we'd finally crested the pass above the Bow Valley. I was happy when Brox insisted we walk around for a few minutes, but climbing off was almost more painful than staying up. Maddy and I dug out a snack and drank from our water sacks. The water tasted like old leather.

"We can see our whole route from here," said Brox. "Behind us, we can see Castle."

It looked huge from here, and very much like a castle, perched high above the river valley.

"If we turn and look ahead, we can see the river valley we'll follow to the Rockwall."

"Where is it?" asked Maddy.

"Right at the end of the valley," said Brox.

I looked down the valley to the mountains blocking the end of it. Instead of a series of mountains lined up in a row, it looked like a solid wall, with the only gaps high along the ridge. "The weavers are at the base of the Rockwall?" I asked, hopeful but doubting.

"No, high up in the clouds." He said it like that would be a beautiful place to live.

I just felt depressed. How were we going to get up there?

Maddy and I stood on a big rock to get back onto Brox and Vivienne. I boosted Maddy and held her while she wiggled into place, and then I threw myself on to Brox's back, grabbed handfuls of fur, and squirmed until I could get one leg over the far side.

Brox snorted and harrumphed, but he stayed still while I struggled.

As soon as we were settled, he headed down the steep drop into the valley. I leaned back, gritting my teeth as sore spots rubbed.

Vivienne began to sing:

> *Come, follow follow follow,*
> *follow follow follow me.*
> *Whither shall I follow follow follow,*
> *whither shall I follow follow thee?*
> *To the greenwood, to the greenwood,*
> *to the greenwood, greenwood tree.*

"We should sing this as a round," said Brox.

"What?" asked Maddy. "A round?"

"Indeed," said Brox. "We all sing together; then we divide into three groups, and all start at different times."

Maddy giggled. "That would sound terrible!"

"No, no," said Brox. "We start at precise moments, so the sounds all fit together." He paused, and said in a soft voice, "It would make Vivienne very happy."

Maddy's mouth twitched. "Then we should definitely do it. How do we divide in three?"

I sagged. "Maddy," I muttered.

"We'll sing," she said, laughing at me. "Josh, when are you ever in all your life going to have another chance to sing rounds with buffalo?"

I started to grin in spite of myself.

Vivienne organized us. "First, we'll sing all together. Then, um, Maddy – you'll be first. I'll start with you to help you get going. Then Josh and Brox together – Josh, you'll have to sing loudly. I'm afraid Brox cannot carry a tune."

I coughed to cover my laugh. This was going to be a disaster.

"I'll come in third." She sang the song for us, and then we joined her, all together. Then, conducting with her head, she gestured for Maddy to begin.

Brox definitely couldn't carry a tune, but he made up for it in volume. We followed each other through the song, around and around, until we were too tired to continue.

We kept moving as we sang, down towards Storm Mountain. The crows kept their distance, distressed by Brox's singing.

Trees blocked our view of the Rockwall as we descended into the valley, and then it disappeared entirely as snow began to fall. Fat flakes drifted down, landing lightly on our hair and eyelashes. Soon we were coated in gleaming white.

The clouds thickened, the sky darkened, and more snow fell. I was mesmerized by the flakes flying at me. They layered on my hair and my eyelashes and melted on my cheeks.

Brox plodded on. I couldn't tell if he knew exactly where he was going, or if he was just walking because there was nothing else to do.

I didn't want to say anything. Even after singing together, I still felt intimidated by the buffalo. But we couldn't ride through the storm all night. "We need to find shelter," I said.

"We're almost there," said Brox.

"At the Rockwall?" Maddy asked.

"No," he said, snorting. "That's for tomorrow. We're almost at your shelter for the night." He looked up at the sky, flakes falling into his eyes. "Corvus," he bellowed. "Corvus!"

Nothing. The snow muffled even his voice.

"Ah, well, we'll find them," said Brox, as he plodded on.

He headed down to a stream, crashing through bushes and pushing his nose into snowy banks. When cliffs rose above the stream, Brox harrumphed in satisfaction. "Almost there."

Then an otter-person jumped up and whacked him on the nose. "*Ssst!* That is close enough!"

Brox snorted and backed into Vivienne, who stumbled into the stream. Maddy shrieked and clung to snow-slicked fur.

The otter-person wasn't as tall as Greyfur, but she had the same grey hair across her head and shoulders. She said, "Crows told us you were coming. *Ssst!* You are not welcome here."

"The children need a warm place to spend the night," said Brox, calm but insistent.

"*Humans* are not welcome," she said.

More otter-people emerged out of the storm and gathered around the first, watchful and wary. Crows joined us, too, quietly settling on snow-covered branches.

I didn't want to push in where we clearly weren't wanted, but the storm was getting worse and Maddy and I needed a safe place to sleep. I shook the snow off my head, wiped my face, and said, "We need to learn how to repair the veil. It is the Will of the Gathering." I didn't need any proof – magic resonated in my words.

The otter-people froze, only their eyes moving as they looked back and forth among themselves. Finally the grey-haired otter-person said, "You believe you can fix veil?"

"That is his task," said Brox.

"*Sssst!* Will he succeed?"

"No other can," said Brox, snorting softly.

"But –"

Vivienne interrupted. "He needs our help."

"Very well," said the otter-person. "*Chrrr.* They may come in. But only the humans. None others, *tss.*" She glared at the crows.

Brox and Vivienne nodded, but the crows cawed in a clamour. She ignored them. When they settled on the trees and bushes nearest the cave, she frowned. They glared back.

I slid off Brox's back and staggered, my legs stiff from the ride, my back aching, my shoulders throbbing. I caught Maddy and steadied her as she struggled to keep her balance on wobbly legs. Then we pulled down our bags and our blankets and shook off as much snow as we could.

"No buffalo furs, *sssst!*" said the otter-person, her nose turned up. "They are too smelly."

Brox grunted. "They're humans. They need blankets for warmth."

Sighing, she nodded again, and gestured for us to enter her cave, a dark opening in the cliff wall.

"Will you be all right in the storm?" I asked Brox. "You and Vivienne and the crows?"

Brox snorted with laughter, a rough *hoff hoff.* "Of course. We do not need caves. We will be fine. We will stay nearby, and make sure Gronvald doesn't come."

I shivered – I'd forgotten about Gronvald. Trusting that Aleena and the crows would warn us if he did show up, I followed Maddy inside.

The cave was musky and dark and warm. Woven grass mats covered the floor, and baskets and pouches of reed and grass were set along the walls.

A crowd of otter-people followed us in. They collected their things and left quietly, leaving us alone with the grey-haired otter-person, a younger otter-woman almost as tall as me holding a baby, and two small otter-children.

"This is my daughter Reynar," said the grey-haired one, "and her children, *hnn*. Baby Folens, and twins Drenba and Dreylac." Reynar had rich red-brown fur and pale skin, as did little Folens. The twins' fur was bright red-gold, and their skin had a golden sheen.

Reynar nodded, but said nothing. The twins peeked at us from behind her. Maddy smiled at them and they ducked out of sight.

"I am Greyfur," said the grey-haired otter-person.

"Greyfur?" asked Maddy. "We know another Greyfur."

"*Chrrr*. You are lucky," she answered. "Greyfur is name of respect for all old enough to have grey hair." She pointed to a corner of the cave vacated by those who'd left. "You may sleep there."

We placed our bags and blankets on the mats, and started to strip off our snowy outerwear.

Greyfur said, "Leave clothes, *tss*. Eat first, outside. We do not light fires inside!" I could hear Eneirda's scorn of humans in her voice.

Somehow the otter-people had managed to light a fire in the snowstorm, tucked out of the wind against the cliff wall. Soon they were grilling fish threaded on sticks – small trout, I guessed.

Maddy and I were ravenous. Although we don't usually like fish, we devoured this. The otter-people ate, too, but they ate their fish raw.

The small fire provided enough light to find our way back to the entrance to the cave, but once inside it was too dark to see. Maddy and I stumbled around until, finally, we stood still in the middle of the cave.

"What is wrong?" asked Greyfur.

"It's dark," said Maddy.

"Yes, *hnn*. Is night. Is not dark in human world at night?"

I laughed. "Yes, of course it is, but we have lights. We don't see well in the dark," I explained, finally understanding the problem.

"*Hnn*," she said. "Humans."

"Josh, could you use your firestone?" Maddy asked.

"Would that be okay?" I asked Greyfur.

"If magic to spare, better to warm cave for Folens."

There was so much unsaid in her sentence, but without being able to see her face, I couldn't interpret it. If I had magic to spare – did that mean they did not? They didn't have enough magic to keep their babies warm?

I pulled the firestone out of my pocket and let magic flow into it, just enough for a soft glow. Maddy and I found our corner, and pulled off our jackets. It was warmer than outside, but not warm enough for little children.

The twins stared as we peeled off layers of clothes, curiosity and horror in their eyes. Maddy laughed and held out a mitten. Hesitantly, they touched it. She slipped it on her hand, took it off again, and gave it to them. They took turns trying it on.

While they played, I let magic fill my body and radiate throughout the cave. As I thought of warmth, the air temperature slowly rose, until a gust of wind from outside blew past it. I walked to the entrance to the cave and drew a barrier of magic just thick enough to stop the wind.

When I turned back the twins were staring at Maddy, eyes huge, mouths open. Maddy was kneeling beside them, coaxing the elastic out of her ponytail. Slowly, she ran her fingers through her hair, working out the tangles. Drenba and Dreylac crept closer, fascinated.

While they stroked her hair, Maddy studied the cave. "Josh," she said, "they have baskets. That's a kind of weaving."

"Yes," I said. I ran my hands around a small basket filled with berries, and then over a woven mat, feeling the vertical and horizontal lines weaving around each other. Then I studied the weaving through Maddy's ring. "This has a different magic than in the veil. It's plain, purposeful, solid. It doesn't have any of the delicacy of the veil." I turned to Greyfur. "Can you weave anything finer than this?"

"What for?"

"For the veil. To repair the veil."

"No, *tss*. Veil far beyond our skills, *hnn*."

The baby woke and stretched, and then scrunched up his face and cried. Reynar nursed him while Greyfur watched, her face tight.

"Folens sick," she said. "I will make his medicine, *hnn*. But it will not be enough."

"What's wrong with him?" Maddy asked.

"*Sssst!* Not enough magic," said Greyfur. "Our babies grow well with magic. Without it, they struggle." She sighed. "*Tss*, will be difficult winter for many families."

When Reynar had finished nursing Folens, Greyfur took him and rocked him gently. "*Chrrr*, check on others," she said. Reynar nodded and slipped out of the cave, looking relieved to be away from us for a little while.

When Folens started to fuss, mewling softly, Greyfur handed him to me and began to rummage in the baskets along the back wall of the cave. I stared at the baby in shock. He stared back, equally surprised. He opened his mouth to wail, and then sighed instead, and nestled against me.

"He likes your magic, *hnn*," said Greyfur, smiling slightly as she laid a shallow basket on the mat in front of me. Several kinds of dried leaves lay in the basket beside one shriveled, dark muskberry. We'd eaten fresh muskberries last summer, before we realized they were a source of magic that magic folk didn't like to share with humans. Fresh, they were a deep purple-red, and tangy. Dried, they looked almost black.

She placed the leaves in her mouth and chewed them into a small lump. Then she added the muskberry, chewing lightly and carefully. She scooped the paste out of her mouth and touched a finger to Folen's lower lip. When his mouth opened, she slipped in the paste, and held a finger to his chin to force his mouth closed. He grimaced and sniffed, but slowly sucked on it.

Greyfur watched him carefully. "There is enough for one muskberry every day, *tss*. To make up for magic fading. But there is not enough to last until fresh berries grow." She looked at me "Running out will not matter, if you fail. He will not live that long."

Folens finally swallowed, relaxed and drifted into sleep. I held him out to Greyfur, but she shook her head. "He is comfortable with you. Your magic is good for him."

So I held the baby while Greyfur tidied, and Maddy and the twins played. When Reynar returned, she was horrified to see me holding Folens. She rushed over, but Greyfur stopped her with a sharp, "*Sssst!* Folens likes his magic."

Folens woke and shifted; a little four-fingered hand reached up and grabbed the edge of my shirt. Then he slept again.

Maddy studied him through her ring. "Magic is flowing from you into him," she said. "Just a little, but he has so little."

When it was time for bed, Greyfur settled me in my fur blanket with Folens still cradled in my arms. Reynar hovered, but Greyfur chased her off. "*Chrrr*, tonight you can sleep. Folens will be well."

The twins cuddled in with Maddy, like puppies in a tangle.

I lay awake holding Folens, his hand tight around one of my fingers. I wondered if I was going to be able to save him, or if he would die this winter, while his family grew colder and weaker without the magic they needed.

CHAPTER SEVEN

TO THE ROCKWALL

REYFUR WOKE US BEFORE DAWN, shifting sleepy children so we could stand and pull on our boots and jackets. The storm had cleared, leaving an icy world coated in white. Slowly the sky began to lighten as we ate a breakfast of grilled fish.

"They must think we're total pigs," said Maddy, looking at the piled skewers of fish they'd cooked for us.

Brox insisted we eat it all. "We cannot provide lunch, and what Keeper packed must last."

So we ate everything. Then we washed our hands in the stream to clean off the smell of fish, and splashed our faces. The icy water shocked us fully awake.

The crows sat quietly, lined up along tree branches, but I could feel their anxiety, their desperate need to move. It made me twitchy too.

We loaded our bags on Brox and Vivienne and I hoisted Maddy up from a big rock. I tucked her robe around her and handed her mine to hold for a minute. Then I wrestled myself onto Brox's back.

Maddy dug around in her bag and pulled out her fur hat. She flipped it so the fur was on the inside, and handed it to Reynar. "For Folens. To sleep in on cold nights."

"*Chrrr.* Thank you," she said softly, and smiled just a little.

Finally, we headed out, back to the river that would lead us to the Rockwall. "Thank you," we called over our shoulders.

"They'll be back for another night on the way home," said Brox.

The crows flew in circles around us, restless and ready to be underway.

Riding a second day was more painful than anything we'd done the day before. Every muscle screamed, and every sore spot complained. But the view soon made me forget the pain. Everything was covered in gleaming white. The trees were dusted with snow, tree stumps looked like mushrooms with caps of white, and rocks were softened into mounds. Only the river itself was free of snow, a clear light blue except for the ice along the shore.

Sunrise lit the clouds in pale pink. It brightened as

it hit the mountain peaks, and then crept down the slopes of the mountains. When the sun hit the snow, it was blindingly white.

As the sun rose, the snow began to melt. Sparkling water droplets formed on the tips of leaves and splashed to the ground. Clumps of snow fell from the trees in soft *thwumps*.

"Quiet, now," said Brox.

Maddy and I looked up. I gestured to the crows to be silent.

Softly, he said, "We don't want to wake her."

"Wake who?" asked Maddy. I could hear the nervousness in her voice.

"The ochre monster," said Vivienne. "We do not want to wake the ochre monster."

"Humans call her the Paint Pots, puddles of ochre mud," said Brox. "But she is not puddles. She is an ancient monster. She sleeps now, unless something wakes her. Humans made her very angry when they mined ochre. She does not like humans. So we must not wake her."

I remembered hiking to the Paint Pots, a short walk above the river we were following. They'd looked like pools of mustard-coloured mud, thick and oozy. I couldn't imagine that was a being. Or that it could hurt us. But Maddy and I rode in absolute silence, barely even breathing, until we were far down the valley.

We rode along the river on a wide gravel bed.

Riding on the flat was a relief to our sore back and stomach muscles, but the rubbing continued.

The river widened and deepened, icy blue and cold. Vivienne started a new song:

> *My paddle's keen and bright,*
> *flashing with silver,*
> *swift as a wild goose flight,*
> *dip, dip and swing.*

> *Dip, dip and swing her back,*
> *flashing with silver,*
> *swift as the wild goose flies,*
> *dip, dip and swing.*

"But you can't paddle," I said to Brox.

"Ah well, Vivienne likes to imagine," he said. "Right now, she's probably flying down a river in a canoe, sunlight flashing on the water drops falling off the end of the paddle." He smiled. "This is why we like to travel. Such wonderful experiences."

As we walked, the Rockwall became visible again, slowly growing as we neared it, into a massive wall of rock blocking our path. When we finally reached its base, Brox stopped beside a stream pouring into the river. He said, "This is as far as we go. It's too steep for us after this."

"So what do we do?" I asked, feeling queasy. Going

on without Brox and Vivienne seemed much worse than travelling with them.

"Follow the stream up the mountain," he said, pointing one hoof into the forest above us. Then he pointed with his nose high up on the Rockwall, to a ridge between two peaks. "The path will take you to a lake. Follow the shore of the lake to the left, and around. The weavers are on the far side."

"And the guardian?" Maddy asked.

Brox shifted his weight, uncomfortable. "I know nothing about the guardian. I am sorry."

"What about Gronvald?" I said.

Brox and Corvus spoke, then Brox translated. "They've seen nothing of him yet, but Aleena has told them he is tracking you."

My stomach churned.

Brox snorted. "He'll wait and watch. The crows will tell you if he comes near."

Maddy and I ate lunch, drank from the river, and refilled our water sacks. I reset the straps on our bags so they'd fit us, folded the buffalo fur blankets and tucked them under a log beneath a huge tree. Hopefully they'd stay dry.

"We'll wait for you here," said Brox.

"How long will you wait?" I asked.

"Until you return."

"What if something goes wrong?"

"Nothing will go wrong," he said.

At the same time, Vivienne said, "The crows will tells us."

Corvus cawed in agreement.

With a cloud of crows leading the way, Maddy and I started up the path along the stream into a dark, silent forest. We hiked up and up, unable to see past the trees. Maddy spotted a chipmunk with two stripes down its back and a thin twitchy tail. It watched us hike past before it raced away. We met a young deer, all leggy and shy. Maddy let out a soft little, "Ohh," and the deer leapt into the forest.

"Do you really think Gronvald is tracking us?" Maddy asked, checking over her shoulder.

"The crows will let us know," I said, distracted. I was more worried about what we'd find when we arrived at the Rockwall. I began to hum again, softly:

Come, follow follow follow,
follow follow follow me.
Whither shall I follow follow follow,
whither shall I follow follow thee?
To the Rockwall, to the Rockwall,
to the Rockwall...

What rhymed with *thee?* And then I had it. *To the Rockwall, then we'll see.* I swallowed and stopped singing.

The snow deepened as we climbed higher. Soon the slope was so steep the path cut back and forth in switchbacks. Maddy and I plodded on, eyes on our feet, trying not to think about how far we had to go. An occasional caw from a crow reminded us we weren't totally alone, but it wasn't much comfort.

We snacked on Halloween candy and drank carefully, until the path neared the stream again. The crows cawed, circling around us as we climbed down to the water. We ignored them while we drank and filled our water sacks.

When I turned to climb the slope back to the path, Maddy grabbed me. "Something's not right." She pulled out her ring and studied the hillside. "That rock," she said, pointing to the top of the slope.

It was an odd rock, taller than it was wide, with knobby sides. As we watched, the edges shifted and softened. Then Gronvald appeared as his disguise dissolved around him.

As soon as he was visible, the crows descended in a squawking fury. I raised a hand for quiet, and they flew above us, silent.

Gronvald grinned. He stood planted in the centre of the path, towering above us, beside a pile of rocks I knew he could use as weapons.

I swallowed, and tried to speak. "I, uh..." My voice failed. I cleared my throat and tried again. "We are here by the Will of the Gathering," I said.

He winced and took a small step back, but he looked angry. "I do not care!" Gronvald growled.

"Humans have no place in our world."

Maddy shivered.

But he didn't step forward, didn't reach for a rock.

We stared at each other, no one moving.

Finally, I muttered, "I don't think he's going to try to stop us now. He's just trying to scare us. He'll wait until we find a way to repair the veil. Do you think we could walk past him?"

"No," said Maddy, whimpering slightly. "Let's go another way. I'm not sure the Will of the Gathering can hold all that anger."

"Stay with him," I said to the crows.

The crows circled low over the path, blocking Gronvald from following us. He didn't seem to care, as if scaring us was all he wanted, for now.

We turned our backs on the glowering troll, and hiked further up the stream. Then we clambered up the steep side of the valley to meet the path higher up the mountainside. Except we couldn't find the path.

We searched from the valley edge out into the forest and back again, but we couldn't spot it.

"Should we go back?" Maddy asked.

I shuddered.

Maddy spoke again, but crows began cawing so loudly I couldn't hear her. "Corvus!" I snapped, annoyed.

They kept cawing. When I looked up, Crowby flew past my face, a wing smacking my head.

"Ow!" I cried.

Maddy laughed.

She landed right in front of us, muttering in a low grumble. While I was struggling to understand, Maddy laughed again and pointed to a second crow, perched on a branch a few feet away. A third waited in line a little further up the slope.

"They're showing us the way," said Maddy.

So we followed the crows. As soon as we reached one, cawing from a branch, and thanked him, another started cawing further up the mountainside.

"Josh, this is how the magpie parents in our garden called to their little babies to come to them." She smiled, delighted. I didn't find the idea as charming as Maddy did.

They led us back to the path and on up the mountain. We grew hot and thirsty, even though the air was cold and the ground white with snow. We tied our jackets around our waists, and shoved hats and mitts into our bags.

After an afternoon of pain, climbing more and more slowly as the altitude tired us, we finally crested the ridge. We could see the Rockwall looming high above us, and a clear blue lake cradled in snow below. The low sun cut across the face of the Rockwall at a steep angle, lighting ridges and triangles of rock. It was stunningly beautiful, radiant with magic. I wanted to stand there and drink it in, to hold the moment forever.

"Around the lake?" Maddy asked. She looked tired.

"In a minute," I said. "Let's rest a bit."

"We'll get cold."

"I know. Just for a few minutes."

I brushed snow off a fallen log. We perched on it while I dug out a wedge of cheese and one of Keeper's huge buns. We ate and drank and rested, and once we started to feel the cold, we stood, creaking and sore, not at all ready to push on.

"Around the lake," I said, eyeing the low sun and the narrow path. "We need to hurry."

The sun dipped below the mountain, lighting the far side of the valley but leaving us in deep shade. I shivered – we'd die without shelter. We had to find the weavers and get past their guardian. Even thinking about that made me feel weak. I sucked in a breath and kept walking.

The crows flew with us. If we paid attention, at least we'd know if Gronvald showed up. That should have been reassuring, but somehow I felt like we were being watched.

We passed some berries near the path, clusters of small creamy white balls on low bushes. Each berry had a tiny black dot on the tip; they looked like eyeballs, watching. *That's just silly*, I thought. But I felt uneasy.

"Gronvald?" I asked Corvus.

He cawed casually.

I guessed that meant no. And still I felt it.

We found more berries as we followed the curve of the lake to the face of the Rockwall. I watched them as we walked by. The dark centres slowly turned, watching us.

The path narrowed, squeezed between the lake and the Rockwall. And then it stopped, blocked by a pile of snow.

I stepped closer, and the snow erupted. I gasped and Maddy shrieked as a cat leapt out, huge and totally silent. The crows flew up in a flurry of panicked squawks. The cat swatted at the crows, and then stopped and slowly licked one paw. It was completely white, large and powerful. It watched us with eyes the cold blue of glacial ice. Finally it turned and walked up the path ahead of us.

As my heart slowed its frantic drumming, I checked with Maddy. "You okay?"

She nodded, looking pale. "Is that the guardian?" she asked.

"I have no idea," I said.

The crows settled on branches near us, Corvus beside me. He cawed once.

"Yes, we need to hurry," Maddy said.

Corvus cawed again, still sitting on the branch.

Maddy and I looked around at all the crows clustered on nearby trees.

"This is as far as you'll take us, isn't it?" I asked, my voice tense.

Corvus cawed once more, one sharp caw.

Yes, he meant. I took a deep breath. "We must be almost there," I said to Maddy. "That's good news, right?"

She smiled weakly, but said nothing.

I nodded to the crows, took Maddy's hand, and stepped around the curve in the path, away from the lake.

That's where we met the guardian. Not the cat, the suddenly lovely, wonderful cat. The guardian was a spider. A giant spider, long and creamy white, dangling from a thread in front of a door. The door was a solid arched slab of wood, set into the side of the mountain. I couldn't see any way to open it. Besides, how could we reach it, with a giant spider slowly spinning on its thread, silently watching us?

CHAPTER EIGHT

THE WEAVERS

THE SPIDER WAS – TALL? LONG? BIG? Whatever the term, there was a lot of it. It was taller than me, with long thin legs, a multi-parted body and far too many eyes. Horrified, I counted six, all black and shining. I swallowed, and backed into Maddy. She clung to my arm, barely breathing.

Shadows of long thin legs reached down the door, with another set reflected in blue on the snow below.

For a moment I forgot all of that in awe at its beauty. It was incredibly delicate, pale and mottled in cream, light browns and greys. How could I capture the soft colours? I'd need translucent watercolours – Paynes grey and burnt sienna, perhaps. Then I looked into its six eyes and shuddered.

It spun on its thread, watching us through all its eyes as it turned. Slowly it descended, letting out thread to reach the ground. It looked at me, and then at Maddy, as it stretched its legs to the earth.

I could feel panic swamping me, making me want to run, to hide, to throw up. How could we fight this? I began to draw magic into myself. I didn't know what I'd do with it, but I had to be ready.

Maddy stood beside me, staring, frozen.

Horrible spider scenes from my favourite movies played in my head. I shook them off and refocused on magic.

Maddy bumped my arm. I glanced up to see her walking straight to the spider. "Maddy!" I cried, and reached for her.

Just beyond my grasp, she stepped up to the spider and bowed, smiling. Then she held out a hand. "Hello."

The spider laughed and shook itself. All its long legs and eyes and strange body parts rearranged themselves into a person wearing a spider-pale cloak. He was a very tall, very thin man, with long, pale blonde hair, and fair skin almost translucent in the light reflected off the snow. His eyes were a soft grey. He stared at us curiously.

That's when I remembered the Gathering. "We need to see the weavers," I said. "It is the Will of the Gathering."

The man laughed. "You don't need to invoke the

Will of the Gathering. Anyone who can see us is welcome." He bowed to Maddy. "That takes a magic very few have."

"I don't have any magic," said Maddy. "Only a ring." She held up her finger.

"Well, you must see very clearly," he said, "to see me without using that ring."

I stared at Maddy, suddenly realizing she hadn't been looking through it. "How did you do that?" I asked.

"I'm not sure. I could just *see*, you know?"

No, I didn't know. My magic was different.

"I am Dorshan," said the man, as he placed his long thin hand on the door and gently pushed. It swung open at his touch, even though such a large door must be heavy. He bowed, and we stepped in. We could hear a frenzy of crows cawing as the door slid shut behind us with a soft *thunk*.

We walked into a light-filled cathedral. That was my first impression, at least. Then I realized I was wrong; it was an incredibly simple hallway, just stone walls and tall windows, but the light gleamed off the cream stone walls and it felt...it felt peaceful, deeply quiet, like a monastery.

From the door, the hallway curved along the front face of the mountain, with windows fitted to follow the lines of the rock. Through every window we could see mountains and evening sky, making the stone hall feel light and airy. When I commented on it, Dorshan said, "Of course. The hall is woven of mountain and sky."

"How is that possible?" Maddy murmured.

I shook my head.

The cat that had startled us outside walked with us, like a pet cat, except it was large enough for Dorshan to rest his hand on its head while they walked.

"This is Menolee," said Dorshan. "We wanted to call her Snow Ball but that seemed too obvious."

Menolee meowled, a wild cry that echoed off the ceiling.

Dorshan led us down the hall, pausing to let us study tapestries hung along the inside wall. Some shimmered like dew, others sang with rich deep colours. A few brooded, dark as storms. The more I looked, the more I wondered what they were woven from.

"We can weave anything," said Dorshan, as if he could read my mind.

A wave of joy washed over me. If the weavers could weave anything, they could repair the veil.

Dorshan continued. "My favourite task is weaving the first leaves into new robes." His face lit up, bright with memories of spring.

Weavers passed us as we studied the tapestries – they were all tall and lean and simply dressed. Menolee butted her head against the hand of each weaver who walked by. The weavers nodded politely to us and to Dorshan, but no one spoke. They felt as quiet as the hall.

We followed Dorshan as the hall curved around the mountain. He led us to a small alcove. "We have visitors," he announced to the three weavers sitting by a stone fireplace. They looked surprised.

"We rarely see anyone but the birds," said a tall, thin, white-haired woman, in a pale robe coloured with a hint of apricot. She stood, and her robe rustled softly around her. "I am Eldest," she said, holding out a hand in welcome.

"This is Aloshius the Elder," she said, gesturing to her right.

The second weaver nodded and smoothed his robe with long, narrow hands. His hair was pale gold, barely darker than the faint gold of his robe.

"And Lyatha," Eldest continued, holding out a hand to her left.

Lyatha, dressed in a robe of peach and cream, smiled, her soft blue eyes sparkling. "Welcome," she said. "Come, warm yourself by the fire." Her hair was pale silver, and her skin almost translucent. I felt that if I watched long enough I would see through her skin to the blood pumping in her veins.

As Lyatha helped us out of our winter clothes, Eldest thanked Dorshan and he left, returning to guard duty, I assumed.

When we leaned down to take off our boots, Maddy whispered, "They're barely there, Josh. I checked through my ring to be sure."

"Like ghosts?" I asked, feeling shocked.

"No, not ghosts." She hesitated. "Just...just thin." She frowned, struggling to describe it. "More spirit than flesh," she finally announced.

I could feel her shiver. I swallowed, and spoke. "We are here by the Will of the Gathering."

Lyatha held up a hand to stop me. "You have come a long way. You shall bathe and change, and then share a meal with us. Then you may tell us the needs of the Gathering."

Eldest and Aloshius nodded in agreement, their smiles sweet and gentle, but at the same time a little withdrawn, as if they weren't used to company.

Lyatha, Maddy and I collected our jackets and bags, and continued down the hall. Lyatha led us to a curved door set between two tall windows. We followed her down a short flight of stairs into a small room. It was a simple, sparsely furnished room, with two stone ledges piled with beautifully woven bedding to sleep on, a stone shelf under a wall of windows and a small stone fireplace. But out the windows, the sky and the mountains were so huge the room felt enormous.

Lyatha knelt and lit a fire with such ease she must have used magic. The fire warmed the room as she lit candles. She carried one through a small door beside the stairs. When she returned, she said, "The bathing room. I'll bring robes for you. Take your time. Someone will come when it is time to dine."

Maddy bathed first, while I lay watching the sky darken. Then, to keep myself awake, I squirmed around so I could see the tapestry covering the wall behind our beds. It was a mountain meadow filled with blooms, but it was so vibrant I wondered if the weavers had woven the flowers themselves into the tapestry.

I'd been consumed by worry, about repairing the veil and keeping Maddy and me safe. Now I started to relax. The weavers could fix the veil, and they would look after us. It felt deeply peaceful here, safe and quiet.

Lyatha had brought woven robes for us to wear, of just the right length. Maddy's was a pale sky blue, soft but not shining. Mine was pure white. Maddy gasped when she saw it.

"You look..." she said. "You look..."

"What?" I said, feeling silly in a long skirt.

"You look...powerful, like you're wearing magic."

We heard a sound at the door, softer than a knock. Maddy opened it to Menolee. "Um, is it time for dinner?" she asked. Menolee yawned.

She led us to a second alcove, warmed by a crackling fire in a stone fireplace. Eldest sat at one end of a long table, with Aloshius the Elder at her right and Lyatha at her left. Maddy and I sat beside them, opposite each other. Menolee stretched out by the fire.

"Will Dorshan be joining us?" I asked, struggling to match the formality of the setting.

"He has returned to guard duty," said Eldest. "He

will eat there."

I wondered if he would eat as a weaver, or as a spider.

"We have a feast to welcome you," said Eldest. "We don't have guests very often. When we do, we try to treat them well."

The food was simple but delicious, and as long as Maddy and I kept eating, the food kept coming – meat cooked with herbs, delicately cut vegetables, woven pastries. We drank what looked like pale wines, but they didn't make Maddy and me silly. My favourite tasted of honey and sunshine on a bright spring morning.

Thick candles lit the table, leaving deep shadows around the edges of the room, except where the light from the fire danced. As we ate, the moon rose and shone through the windows, creating new shadows.

The weavers ate lightly, simply tasting each dish, but they encouraged us to have as much as we wanted. When our stomachs were tight and round, we stopped, sighing.

Then, finally, the weavers asked why we were in the magic world and Maddy told them our story.

When she finished, Eldest said, "And what do you need from us?"

"We need to fix the veil," I said. "I mean, you do. To weave it, to repair the tears."

"We cannot," said Eldest.

Maddy's eyes widened. "What?"

Fear grabbed me, but I pushed it aside. *Of course they can*, I told it.

Eldest sighed. "We are descendants of the Ancient Ones, but we do not have their power. We are weavers, but not of the veil."

"Can't you at least try?" I asked, my stomach twisting.

"We cannot cross the veil. We cannot touch the veil."

"But you have to try!" I cried.

Aloshius the Elder said, "Do you think we have not?" He pushed up the sleeves of his robe, showing dark red scars zigzagging up his arms. "It throws us off. We cannot touch it."

Lyatha pushed up her sleeves, revealing more scars. Eldest did the same; her arms were the worst, covered in a web of raised red lines.

"We cannot touch the veil," she said. "We cannot weave it, cannot repair it, cannot even rest a finger on the veil to listen to the song of the Ancient Ones. We can do nothing to help the magic world." She sounded immensely sad.

"Come," she said, "and I will show you."

We walked with her to the end of the hall, to the largest tapestry we'd seen. Holding up a candle, Eldest lit portions of the story, one after another. It showed the Ancient Ones, all together, weaving the veil. I could see magic flowing through their hands, and threads emerging and working their way into the veil, weaving it around the earth. Magic crackled as they wove.

The Ancient Ones were tall like the weavers, but strong and vibrant, full of colour and power. As we moved down the tapestry, we watched magic flow from the Ancient Ones into the veil. They became paler and thinner, as if they were feeding themselves into the veil. By the end of the tapestry, the Ancient Ones sat exhausted, pale and thin like the weavers, except for the joy on their faces as they looked at the veil surrounding the earth in a mantle of magic.

"We are all that is left," said Eldest. I could hear deep sadness in her voice.

"How awful," said Maddy.

Eldest smiled. "They were content." She paused, and added, "As were we. Until now." She closed her eyes and I could feel the pain of their failure to repair the veil their ancestors had given everything to create.

"So who can fix it?" I asked.

"Only you, Josh. You have something of the Ancient Ones about you, a presence, a strangeness. Only you can fix it."

I wish I could, I thought. I'd give anything to repair it. "Teach me how," I said.

"There is nothing we can teach."

Then it couldn't be repaired.

Now I understood how the veil was made, woven of magic and something of the Ancient Ones themselves, leaving them drained of everything except stillness and a remarkable ability to weave anything except the veil. But they couldn't repair it, and neither could I.

I went to bed in despair, and didn't sleep. I watched the moon travel across the sky, clouds move in, and snow begin to fall. The snowfall became heavier, matching my mood and giving me something new to worry about. I ignored the bigger problem, and focused on the immediate one: how were we going to get back to Brox and Vivienne?

After a generous breakfast I could barely choke down, Maddy and I got ready to leave. Once Lyatha was content that we were well wrapped and our bags properly packed, Eldest stepped forward, fabric draped over one arm.

"These will keep you comfortable, whatever the weather." She slipped a cloak over Maddy's shoulders, softly patterned in grey like the back of a young robin. Eldest pulled up the hood and touched a hand to Maddy's cheek.

Then she handed me mine. It was creamy white, exactly the cream of Dorshan the spider, and it felt as fine as spider's silk. I shuddered as I took it from her. But it settled over my shoulders as if it had always been there, moving as I moved. When I walked, I forgot about the cloak until it swirled around my ankles in a gentle flourish, reminding me of its presence.

We walked down the hall and out the door. Dorshan and Menolee were waiting. Snow was still falling, and silence echoed in my ears.

"How can we get through the snow?" asked Maddy, her voice small.

Dorshan smiled. "Menolee will take care of that. She'll be very happy, today!" He turned to Menolee, and said, "Meno, please clear the trail for Josh and Maddy, all the way to their escort at the base of the mountain."

Menolee yowled, a wild, joyful cry.

Dorshan smiled. "No avalanches, today, Meno. Just clear the path."

Menolee shook her head, and meowed softly. Then she curled herself into a ball and began to roll. Snow on the path stuck to her; she kept rolling, the ball growing larger as more and more snow clung. Soon she was out of sight, leaving a perfectly clear path for us to follow.

"Won't she be awfully big when she gets to the bottom?" Maddy asked.

Dorshan laughed. "She'll shake herself out whenever she gets too big."

Maddy and I said goodbye, and watched while the

weavers returned to their hall. Dorshan stayed outside, on guard duty again.

"Before we go, could we watch you turn into a spider?" asked Maddy.

"Of course. Goodbye, my friends. May the Will of the Gathering keep you safe and help you find your way." He shook himself and the cloak floated around him. "It's all in the weaving, and in my intention. Watch closely."

He seemed to be speaking only to Maddy, so I stepped back.

Maddy watched intently as he twitched his cloak with one hand and a shrug of his shoulders. As it settled, he settled too, smaller and thinner, and suddenly he was a spider again.

Maddy twitched her own cloak as she grinned. "That's so cool," she muttered. Then we turned and started down the path.

After all the magic of the weavers and their hall, the beauty of the fresh morning and the joy of Menolee rolling down the mountain, all I could think was a despairing, *Now what?*

CHAPTER NINE

CROW BY CROW

THE CROWS SWARMED US AS WE CIRCLED the lake. "Settle down," I said. "Settle down. We're fine."

Corvus landed directly in front of me, demanding answers. The others clustered nearby, Crowby on my shoulder. She leaned against my ear and murmured softly.

I touched her head. "No, the weavers can't fix the veil. I have no idea what to do now." I struggled not to snap at them, not to cry.

Corvus flew off immediately. I called after him to stop, but either he didn't hear me or he chose to ignore me. *Now everyone will know*, I thought, as we trudged down the mountain.

Maddy and I walked in silence. The trip down was faster than hiking up, but it wasn't long before my knees reminded me of how hard it is to hike down a mountain.

We never saw Menolee, but we knew she'd rolled by. The path was perfectly clear. Every so often we'd pass an explosion of snow scattered across the forest, with a fresh path straight through the middle.

As we walked all I could think about was my failure. I remembered how Folens had felt snuggled in my arms, his fingers holding mine while he slept. I'd failed him. I'd failed the weavers with their veil-scarred arms. I'd failed the entire magic world. How could I go home knowing this world was suffering?

Brox and Vivienne were waiting by the river. They must have heard from Corvus how I'd failed. They didn't say anything – they just waited, huffing softly, while we dug the buffalo robes out of the snow, strapped on our bags, and climbed up. We tucked the robes around our legs where our cloaks couldn't reach, but I knew we wouldn't get cold. The cloaks had been light as we hiked down the mountain but as soon as we stopped moving they snuggled around us, warm and comforting.

My only other comfort was that Brox and Vivienne must have sensed my mood. Brox talked with Maddy, and Vivienne sang, but they let me sit in silence.

We headed upriver, north up the long valley back to the otter-people.

Now that I understood how the veil was woven, I could almost feel it in my hands. I kept flexing my fingers, running my hands up and down imaginary threads, picturing myself being able to pull the broken threads together and reweave them.

"I need to find a doorway," I said to Brox.

Maddy looked up, a flash of hope in her eyes. "You have an idea?"

I shook my head. "No. I just – I just want to touch the veil again." My hands twitched. I waved them at Maddy. "Just touch it."

She nodded, and let the eagerness fade from her face. "I understand."

"There's a doorway near the bank of the river," said Brox. "We'll be there soon."

I was content to wait, to ride and be quiet and wait. It felt better than despair, although despair was never far away.

When we reached the doorway, Maddy and the buffalo stayed near the river, letting me work alone. I breathed in magic, letting it fill me. Then I breathed out, and opened the doorway. There was no tear here, but I could see the veil. I touched it, laying my hands on the soft threads. I could feel the tears, feel the history of the veil, hear the song of the Ancient Ones as they wove themselves into the veil. But I could not repair the tears. I didn't have the magic for that.

"Anything?" asked Maddy as I joined her. I shook

my head.

Corvus landed in front of us, holding a piece of paper in his beak. Maddy knelt and took it from him. She unfolded it, choked out a laugh, and handed it to me. Keeper had scrawled in black charcoal, in what looked like a five-year-old's printing:

~~Grfal~~ ~~Grenfol~~ Troll traking you. Bewar.

"We met him on the trail," I said, looking back at the Rockwall.

Maddy shuddered.

"We're not afraid of him," said Brox.

But I knew Gronvald. Just because they weren't afraid of him didn't mean they shouldn't be.

We ate a little, Maddy and me from our bags, Brox and Vivienne grazing on the grasses near the river, periodically lifting their great heads to sniff. We ate quickly, watching for Gronvald.

Vivienne sniffed and froze, her nostrils twitching. Brox joined her, searching for a scent. "Wolves," Brox muttered.

Maddy walked to the edge of the water, looking through her ring.

We heard a howl upriver. We all turned, struggling to see into the forest. When we turned back, we were surrounded by wolves.

Maddy stood alone, separated by the wolves from

the buffalo and me. Three circled her, while the others kept us away. They were huge, seven in all, in shades of grey. Their eyes gleamed yellow as they stared. Maddy moaned in fear.

Vivienne bellowed and raced towards Maddy. A dark wolf leapt at her, his jaws snapping at her leg. Vivienne kicked him and sent him flying, whimpering. A smaller wolf sprang from behind, clawing Vivienne's back. Brox roared and attacked, but two wolves closed in on Maddy.

"No!" I yelled, leaping towards her. A wolf lunged at me, snarling. "We come at the Will of the Gathering," I gasped. Somehow, as weak and squeaky as that came out, magic rang in my words. He paused, just long enough for me to suck in a larger breath and yell, "We come at the Will of the Gathering." My voice rang with power.

The wolves growled and circled, but as we faced them, trying to look strong, the circle eased. They stared at us for a moment longer, and then disappeared into the forest.

We pushed on up the valley, Vivienne ignoring the deep scratches down her back, Maddy and me shaking, the crows anxious and irritable.

Vivienne began to sing again, a quiet hummy lullaby. She was starting the second verse when Brox interrupted with a quiet, "Vivienne, dearest."

Maddy and I looked up. Brox never interrupted Vivienne's songs. Even the crows became quiet. Brox tilted his head, listening.

"What is it?" Maddy asked.

"Ssh," he said, standing motionless.

We all froze and listened, the crows silently circling above us.

Burble, I heard. Blorp, burble splat.

Maddy and I stared at each other. "What is it?" she mouthed.

I shrugged. I had no idea.

Blorble. Burp.

"The ochre monster," said Vivienne, her voice tight. "The ochre monster is waking."

I could feel Brox shudder, and I shuddered too. I didn't want to meet anything he was afraid of.

"Josh, Maddy, not one word," said Brox. "Be still. Breathe softly. We want no sounds, no smells, no hint of human. Understand?"

We both nodded, barely moving our chins.

The crows broke into small squabbling groups, always between us and the Paint Pots, creating a shield of sound. Brox and Vivienne walked faster than ever. Maddy and I gritted our teeth and hung on.

WE ARRIVED AT THE OTTER-PEOPLE'S CAMP JUST before sunset.

They brought us dinner but I couldn't eat. Folens

was dying. He lay nestled in Maddy's fur hat, pale and still. I warmed the cave and knelt by him, holding one tiny hand, trying to send him magic. While I worked, I knew that if I couldn't fix the veil, whatever I did now wouldn't matter.

I left Maddy playing quietly with Drenba and Dreylac, and went outside to sit by the fire. Brox and Vivienne joined me, silently watching the flames. Vivienne began to sing, soft and low:

> *O come sit by my side if you love me.*
> *Do not hasten to bid me adieu.*
> *Just remember the Red River Valley,*
> *and the one that has loved you so true.*

I stared into the fire, thinking about the veil and magic. Folens and muskberries. The Ancient Ones.

As I thought about the Ancient Ones and how they gave themselves to create the veil, I realized something. Magic folk talked about me like I was some kind of hero, or should be, but I wasn't. I was the sacrifice. I had to do what the Ancient Ones did. I had to weave myself into the veil.

I wondered what I would become if I could repair the veil. Would I be just a shadow of myself, like the weavers were of the Ancient Ones? I sat with my fear until I knew exactly what it looked like. And what to do.

"Corvus," I called. "Only the crows can help me

now. I need every crow to bring me muskberries. Ask the otter-people, at every camp. Ask anyone who has some. I don't care if they need them to survive the winter. This is the Will of the Gathering. I need every muskberry that the crows can bring before dawn."

Greyfur heard me. She joined me by the fire and handed me a bowl holding a small pile of dried muskberries. "This is all we have. Use them well, *hnn*."

I took them from her knowing that if I failed, Folens would die. That became another fear to push aside.

I sat holding the bowl, waiting, while Corvus conferred with the crows and they all flew away. When Crowby left, too, I almost called out, "No, not Crowby. She's too young." But I stopped myself. This had to be done.

I knew what this would cost them, in exhaustion and failure and possibly death. With a shock I realized I could feel the crows – not just to empathize with them, but to feel as they felt. I must have been doing it for a while, without realizing it. Right now, I could feel their determination to collect muskberries for me, to save their world, whatever the cost to themselves. I let that determination soak into me.

Then I mourned – for their sacrifice, for the sacrifice of the Ancient Ones, for my own.

I waited as the moon rose, adding wood to the fire when it burned low. I waited while the moon crossed the sky, sitting with Greyfur, with Brox and Vivienne nearby. I could feel the crows as they flew and knew exactly when the first would return.

Greyfur greeted him and handed me the pouch of muskberries he carried. I poured them into the bowl and waited for more.

All through the night crows arrived, sometimes with a pouch or a clawful of muskberries, sometimes clutching only one. Each was placed in the bowl.

I sent them all off again, no matter how tired they were. "Keep looking for muskberries — as many as you can bring me by dawn." I knew the cost of what I was asking, but I couldn't let that stop me.

As they returned I could feel their fatigue. Some carried more than one woven pouch or packet made from a folded leaf. They were bringing muskberries collected by crows too exhausted to return.

An hour before dawn, I began to eat. One at a time, slowly chewing each one, I ate muskberries. The dried berries were dark in the firelight, almost black, shrivelled and sticky. They filled my mouth with flavour, tangy and dark, with a heavy scent. As I ate, I could feel magic. But I didn't focus on it, didn't let it build. Not yet. First I had to eat.

Maddy was up before dawn, worrying. "Are you sure, Josh? This seems so dangerous."

"I'm sure," I said.

"But...remember what happened to the Ancient Ones."

I closed my eyes. "I remember," I said, a little gruffly. "Eneirda and Greyfur didn't want to eat too many muskberries."

"I'm not an otter-person."

"No, you're not. You're not even magic folk. You're just a human being. Just a boy, Josh."

"Let the boy do what he must," said Greyfur.

Maddy sniffed and wiped her eyes, her face pale. I could tell from the way they hovered that Brox and Vivienne were worried, too. But still it had to be done.

Vivienne snuffled at Maddy, and Maddy leaned into her, glad of the company. When she got restless she examined her cloak, running a hand down its softness, flipping it and watching it settle around her. Then she'd turn back to me, her face tight. Eventually she slept.

I waited and ate, and waited some more. Just as the sky began to lighten, the last crows arrived, a cluster of exhausted birds flying together. Crowby was the last to stagger in, clutching a single berry. She was embarrassed she only had one, but it was enough.

I held their muskberries in my hand and slowly ate them, one at a time. Then I stood. I could feel magic pulsing through me.

I strode over to Maddy and gently woke her. "I'm ready," I said. Then I turned to the others. "I need a doorway."

Maddy rubbed her eyes and slowly stood, untangling her cloak. "A torn one?"

"No. Any doorway will do."

Greyfur conferred with Brox and Vivienne.

"There is one south along the river, beyond what humans call Marble Canyon," said Brox.

Greyfur said, "Doorway at Storm Mountain is closer, *hnn*."

"But more difficult for humans and for Vivienne and me. Beyond Marble Canyon is easier."

Greyfur nodded in agreement, and helped us climb onto Brox and Vivienne.

We walked south along the river once again, watching the sun rise below a low bank of clouds, past a curve of mountain covered in low bushes and scattered rocks. Beyond it a stream tumbled down the mountain.

"The doorway is beside that stream," said Brox. "Go quietly. The Paint Pots are nearby."

I nodded and turned to climb the bank. I was filled with magic.

A chorus of cawing stopped me. Aleena was stepping out of the river. When she reached the gravel shore, she shook herself. Water flew off as her long hair and cloak spun around her. When she finished, she was completely dry.

"Gronvald is coming," she said as we walked towards each other.

"What can he do?" asked Maddy. "He's compelled by the Will of the Gathering."

I felt through the magic surrounding me to understand. "Remember when he attacked you in his cave?" I said to Maddy. "He's compelled to help me, but his anger is so strong it doesn't protect any of you." I nodded to the crows, Brox, Vivienne, Aleena and Maddy.

"He cannot attack you directly," Brox said, "but he can try to distract you by attacking us."

"We'll take care of him," said Maddy, looking fierce.

"No, you stay with me," I said.

Maddy shook her head. "This is the one thing I can do, Josh."

Reluctantly, I nodded. I walked along the shore until I found a long, thick stick, like a staff. I handed it to Maddy. I knew how small a weapon it was against Gronvald's power, but I had to give her something. And she wouldn't be alone.

She just smiled, a tight, determined smile.

"Gronvald doesn't scare us," said Brox. "We haven't had a good fight in a long time." He grinned. It didn't reassure me.

"We'll keep Maddy safe," said Vivienne.

And so I walked up the hill to the doorway while Maddy and the others waited for Gronvald.

CHAPTER TEN

IN THE VEIL

I FOUND THE DOORWAY NEAR THE BANK OF the stream, outlined in gold. From there, I had a perfect view of Maddy, the staff held firmly in her right hand. Brox and Vivienne stood to either side, each watching a different direction. Aleena waited in the water, trying to catch Gronvald's scent, while the crows circled overhead. I could feel their tension, their alertness, their drive to do whatever was necessary to give me time to fix the veil.

I turned to the doorway and pushed back my cloak. I didn't need to breathe in magic – I was filled with it. I simply exhaled, and the doorway opened.

I reached into the veil and ran my hands over the threads. I could feel each one, and when I reached far enough, I could touch torn ends lifting off the face of the veil. But I still didn't know how to repair them.

I started to sketch, drawing weaving down my pant leg, vertical lines crossing horizontal lines. I drew a tear, a gash in the veil, threads broken and drifting free. Then I drew them coming together and healing. Somehow drawing the threads became a new kind of drawing. I reached into the veil and touched the threads, and knew I could pull them together and mend them.

Satisfied, I paused to check on the others. They were all staring to the side, looking confused. The curve of the hill blocked my view just enough to hide whatever worried them. Should I walk over? Step out of the veil to see?

I closed my eyes for a moment, to think and decide, and found I *could* see, the entire scene laid out as if I was watching from the air above them: Maddy's golden head between Brox and Vivienne's broad backs, Aleena standing in the river, legs braced against the current. They were all staring at the hillside beside them, dotted with rocks.

As I circled overhead, I watched rocks rise from the ground, growing steadily larger until they were as tall as men. Then, slowly, they transformed into trolls. An army of trolls.

I let out a squawk and realized I was a crow; at least, I was seeing through crow eyes. I snapped open my own eyes and checked that I was still me, still Josh, standing in the veil.

The crows were cawing in a raucous frenzy. I remembered the ochre monster and called out to them to be quiet. It was more caw than words, a hoarse croak, but they understood and fell silent.

When I heard Maddy cry out I shut my eyes, and watched with crow eyes again.

The trolls were marching down the hillside, deep thumps reverberating with every step. Maddy gasped and backed into Brox. Aleena stepped further back into the water, afraid to be part of the fight. Could I send a crow to her, to beg for her help? I felt their hatred of Aleena wash over me. She had killed a crow, last summer. They would not beg.

Instead, they spoke to the trolls. In a perfect imitation of Gronvald, a crow said, "Stop." The trolls turned, and paused.

"Keep going," Gronvald yelled.

The trolls stepped forward again.

Another crow, behind them, said, "Wait."

They turned, searching. Who was speaking? Which troll was Gronvald?

"Walk!" Gronvald screamed.

Another crow, far to the right, said, "No," in Gronvald's voice.

Gronvald roared in anger, waved his arms and stepped forward, bellowing, "Now!"

And they followed him down the hillside, the earth

rumbling as they moved, relentlessly descending on Maddy, Brox and Vivienne.

I could see Maddy shaking, but she studied them carefully. "They're not real," she said, her voice quivering. "They're shadows, Gronvald's magic. He made them." Her voice cracking, she asked, "How do we stop him?"

"Only sunshine can stop him completely, turning him to stone until he's been thawed by twelve hours of darkness," said Brox.

I looked up. The sky had become totally overcast, solid with low, dark clouds.

"But Vivienne and I can stop almost anything," he added.

Then we heard a new sound, an odd, burbling walk. It didn't sound like Keeper walking, solid thumps reverberating through the earth. This was huge, but squishy. How could anything be big enough to make that sound?

Aleena turned deadly white. "We've raised the ochre monster." She sounded stunned.

Brox and Vivienne gasped, and backed up.

I saw her before the others could, as she strode up the river valley. She was massive, the largest creature I'd ever seen, twice the height of Keeper. She was huge-shouldered and strong-thighed, and all mud, all drippy ochre-orange mud. It dropped off her as she walked, but it never ran out, and she never got smaller. She just left a trail of orange behind her.

"She's the Paint Pots?" asked Maddy.

"When she's sleeping," said Vivienne.

"How can she hurt us, if she's only mud?"

"She could drown us in mud, freeze us in mud."

"Why would she do that?" Maddy whispered.

"She hates humans."

I settled back into the veil, reaching for torn ends, trying to learn the tears. And watching. Always watching. I heard a low rumble, a deep burbling voice.

"What's she saying?" Maddy asked.

"Listen carefully," said Brox.

As we listened, sounds emerged, burbling words:

Humans bad.
Stop humans.
Humans bad.
Stop humans.

"But we're not bad," said Maddy. "We're trying to help. Josh is trying to –"

"I know," Brox interrupted. "But we have no way to tell her. She's like an angry two-year-old."

"How do we stop her?"

"We will do everything we can, so Josh can concentrate on the veil."

Maybe we should just run away and try again later, somewhere else. Then I remembered I'd eaten all the muskberries and Folens was dying. It had to be now.

I felt desperate to join them, but I had to repair the veil. They were risking their lives to give me time. I took a breath, trying to slow my pounding heart. I reached deep into the veil and searched for the largest tear. There, at Storm Mountain, where Gronvald had yanked it wide. I touched one side of the tear, stretched further and grabbed the other. Magic flared across me, and I jerked back.

On the hillside, Gronvald raised his arms and began to mutter. Each troll lifted a head-sized rock and flung it at Maddy and the buffalo, a wall of stone raining down. They ducked and scrambled clear, the rocks falling just a little short. The trolls simply walked further down the hillside and picked up a new set of rocks.

I had to help them. I closed my eyes and settled into crowness. I could feel crows all around me, the rush of wind against their feathers, the beat of their wings. Then I felt my own wings. My eyes snapped open and I checked my arms – still there, no feathers, no wings sprouting from my shoulders. But when I closed my eyes I could feel wings, long and strong. Wind ruffled every feather.

Calling to the crows, I gathered them together and, in a black cloud, we launched our assault. That's when I understood why a flock of crows is called a murder of crows.

We were terrifying.

We attacked, a wall of black, dive-bombing the trolls, claws and beaks tearing, in a squawking, cawing mass. Except the trolls were stone, and we couldn't hurt them. I could feel the blows as each crow attacked, flinging themselves at the trolls, but it was like smashing against rock.

The trolls dropped their rocks, and instead raised thousands of pebbles and flung them at the crows. Pebbles thudded against their bodies and crows plummeted to the ground. I gasped at the pain, expecting to fall too, but I continued to circle above, watching.

The crows lay totally still. I held my breath, waiting, hoping for any sign of life. Wind caught a wing and ruffled feathers, and I felt a faint stirring. Then slowly, ever so slowly, they began to move, to tuck in wings and awkwardly fly to the safety of nearby trees. But not all of them. I couldn't see Crowby.

The army of trolls lifted large rocks again.

Brox, Maddy and Vivienne were watching the trolls and worrying about the crows. They'd forgotten the ochre monster. But she hadn't forgotten them.

As soon as she was near enough she threw up a wall of mud, like a tidal wave sweeping across the valley. It washed over Maddy and Brox and Vivienne, coating them in thick orange goo, then swept up the hillside, covering the army of trolls.

"Run," Brox shouted at Maddy. He and Vivienne started to race around in circles, cracking the mud as it stiffened. "Run, before the mud hardens."

Maddy paused, confused, and immediately the mud started to thicken. Even as she understood and tried to run, it was encasing her. Then her cloak shivered and the mud fell off in hard bits, shattering around her. She wiped her face with the cloak and the rest of the mud dropped off, leaving her shining and clean in a sea of ochre mud.

The troll army didn't move fast enough. Soon every troll except Gronvald was encased in rapidly drying mud, some with their rocks still held high. Only Gronvald moved, shaking off the mud in a frenzy of anger. Enraged, he walked to a cliff face and began to mutter, preparing to bring down the cliff in an avalanche.

Before he was ready, Maddy roared and ran forward, her staff swinging. I couldn't stand to watch, to not protect her. I stepped forward, out of the veil, but Aleena was faster as she finally joined the fight, racing up from the water, pushing Maddy back towards Brox and Vivienne.

She walked straight to Gronvald, drawing river water with her. Brox bellowed, distracting Gronvald. As he turned, Aleena flung water at Gronvald and a wall of rocks directly behind him, weaving her hands in a spell over the water as it flew. When it hit the rocks, it froze in a wall of ice.

Gronvald had seen it coming and slipped back into

the cliff face. Aleena followed, flowing with the water into the rocks, searching for Gronvald. Water and rocks sprayed from the rock face as they fought.

I reached into the veil again and found the tear. I could feel each strand of the veil, delicate threads of palest blue. I grabbed one broken end and touched it to another. Nothing happened. I tried again with a new thread. Nothing. Then I found the right one, the matching thread. With a shudder, magic flared from one thread to the other, right across my body, as I became part of the flow of magic.

Gronvald and Aleena were still battling inside the rocks, shards of ice and rock chips spewing out of cracks. The ochre monster watched, trying to understand what was happening.

Slowly I tugged the ends towards each other. When they touched, magic flashed and the threads became one. I worked along the tear, thread by thread, slowly finding each match, magic flowing through me as I joined them.

When the first tear was mended I paused again, emerging from the veil just far enough to check on Gronvald and Aleena. The showers of rock and water and ice stopped, and Aleena slipped out of the rock face, covered in rock dust and blood. She sagged against the cliff face, battered and exhausted. Gronvald didn't appear.

I discovered I could work and watch, so with my eyes focused below, my hands touched and healed. I reached in to the next tear and let magic flow through me. Soon, as I touched one broken end, the other would call out to me. I could reach a little further, a little higher, and it would be in my hand, longing to be repaired.

Slowly I found every place the nexus ring had crossed the veil, carried by Gronvald and Aleena, even Maddy and me. I rewove every tear at every doorway.

Then the ochre monster turned on me. I could hear her burbling:

Humans bad.
Human in veil.
Stop human.

Almost too fast to see, she lobbed a giant mud ball at me. It engulfed me, trapping my arms and legs, covering my face. I couldn't move, couldn't breathe. I fought down panic, and then tried to relax into it, to travel with it, like I'd travelled through the earth the last time I'd been in the magic world. Being ochre. Being mud. I didn't need to breathe. I was the earth boy.

All connection to the crows fled – they were terrified of being buried alive. I was fine with it; I loved the deep magic in the earth. I settled into it, a thick, dark world. Then I heard the ochre monster again.

"Earth boy?" she burbled. "Human boy earth boy?" She paused, as if she was thinking about what this meant.

She knew me from when I'd travelled through the

earth? She recognized me?

Earth boy touching veil.
Earth boy.

She stepped up to me as I hung in the veil, and gently sucked off the mud, pulling it back into her own body.

Shaking, I reached into the veil, searching for the last tear.

Gronvald stepped from the rock face, dripping murky wet rock dust. Maddy looked up at me, still working in the veil. She could see I needed more time, and I could see she was determined to give it to me. I shivered as I realized it was her turn for sacrifice.

She flipped up the hood of her cloak, pulled it close, and shook herself. As the cloak settled around her, she became...not invisible, just less...less noticeable, somehow, as the grey of her cloak faded into the grey of the rocks. Then she settled low and started to creep forward, hidden under her cloak. What was she going to do, leap up and yell, "Boo?"

My hands reached and tugged and magic flared, as I started repairing the last tear, thread by thread. Gronvald must have known I had almost succeeded, because now he turned to me, his face dark with hatred.

That's when Maddy stood, directly in his path. But she didn't yell. Instead, somehow, with a twitch of her cloak, she transformed herself into a spider, soft grey like her cloak, Maddy-sized and terrifying.

I knew it was Maddy and still I saw spider and was afraid. It was huge, with too many legs and too many eyes, all focused on Gronvald. He leapt back with a scream of terror and then stood frozen in fear. This would be the perfect moment for a ray of sunlight, but the clouds were solid.

I reached and connected, trying to use whatever time she could give me.

She watched me work, holding Gronvald, waiting. I could see the strain, spider legs quivering, a hint of Maddy showing through like a shadow. *Oh, Maddy*, I thought, *hold him, just a little longer. I'm so close. Just – a – little – longer.*

And then I was done. I raised my head and nodded, and she sighed with relief.

The moment Maddy relaxed, Gronvald broke through his fear, raised a boulder as large as a beach ball and hurled it at Maddy. She screamed and ducked and the spider illusion vanished. The rock sailed over her head and smashed behind her.

With a roar, Gronvald raised a second, larger rock, and flung it even harder. It flew straight at Maddy, too fast for her to jump clear. I screamed, and Brox leapt forward, shielding her. The rock hit his head with an enormous blow.

He staggered and sank to his knees, head down. I

held my breath, waiting for him to fall over, dead, but he shuddered and slowly stood, the side of his face a bloody, pulpy mess.

Blood flew as he shook his head. It looked like he was struggling to see, one eye smashed, the other covered in blood. And still, he looked fearsome.

He blinked and charged Gronvald, his head down, horns gleaming. Before Gronvald could turn or run or lift a rock, he was sailing into the air, straight at me in the veil.

Gronvald smashed into me, crushing the air out of my lungs, but the veil held, shuddering back and forth, crackling with magic. Gronvald struggled, but we were both caught, unable to pull away.

Hanging in the veil, we could see it was weakened, even though I'd repaired the holes. Magic was leaking through the veil itself, a soft golden flow into the human world. Gronvald reached up and touched it.

"Help me," I said. "Help me fix this."

I knew he'd understood, for just a moment, and then he shut it down, his face twisting in hate. He leaned towards me, his hands reaching for my neck.

Below me, I saw the ochre monster fling a huge ball of mud at Gronvald. I ducked, tucking my head against his chest. The mud hit him in an explosion that splattered across his back and up his head. Mud oozed over his hair and into his ears.

I pulled back, watching the look of shock on his face as the mud began to harden.

Gronvald fought it, still determined to stop me. His hands were huge and strong as they settled around my neck. He smiled as he watched me turn red.

I reached into the veil and tried to shift time. The veil moved past me, faster and faster, but I discovered that, filled with magic, I could control it, slow it, search for the perfect moment.

When his hands shifted to get a better grip, I gasped, "It is the will of the gathering."

He flinched but didn't let go.

"It is the Will of the Gathering," I insisted.

He hesitated.

I found the moment I wanted, and shifted time. Then I yanked us both into the human world, in a tangle of troll and boy and sunlight.

Gronvald was almost entirely coated in mud, but sunlight found the tip of his nose, and he turned to stone as the last bit of dripping mud crept over his face. The mud hardened, encasing the stone troll in a layer of deep orange.

I lay panting for a moment, then stepped back through the veil, careful to find the right time.

The ochre monster had been watching for me. Once she saw me safely returned, she walked away, muttering with little burbles of pleasure:

Earth boy fix veil.
Earth boy fix veil.

"She'll sleep now," said Vivienne, calling to me from near the river.

"Where's Gronvald?" Maddy asked.

"He's a mud-covered statue," I said.

"Will he thaw?"

I glanced up at the army of trolls on the hillside. "He's covered in mud. I don't know if it's permanent or not. The sun can't reach him unless the mud washes off. Maybe he'll be there forever."

ALEENA, VIVIENNE AND MADDY TENDED TO BROX. All around us the crows mourned their dead in an eerie silence. I wanted to rest and mourn with them but the veil called me back.

My repairs weren't enough; the veil itself was more fragile than before. Searching the veil into the future, I could feel it shredding.

I stretched out my arms and let magic flow through me. Slowly I rewove it, layering in more magic. It had to protect this world for all of time.

I could hear Maddy and the others walking up the hill, excited by their success. And I could feel their horror when they saw me, blazing with power, arms stretched wide across the veil. To them, I must look like a spider's prey caught in a web.

"Josh, no!" Maddy cried. "Stop!" Tears streamed

down her face.

Crowby landed on her shoulder and muttered gently, and Vivienne softly woofed against her hand. Together they waited, while I wove myself deeper and deeper into the veil.

The crows gathered on the ground, in complete silence. It felt like a funeral, like maybe they thought it was mine, but they didn't try to stop me. It felt more like they were honouring me.

I rewove every hole, every worn spot, making the veil strong again, the way the Ancient Ones made it. Then I did more. I wove the veil deeper and tighter, so that human changes could never touch the magic world. And then it was enough and I closed my eyes and sank into the veil.

CHAPTER ELEVEN

DREAMING

I DREAMED OF MADDY SOBBING. BROX INJURED, Vivienne tending him. The crows lined up in front of the veil, heads bowed. They were as silent as they'd been for their crow funeral, like they were mourning the dead.

Aleena watched tears roll down Maddy's face. As she watched, tears leaked out of her own eyes and crept down her cheeks. She touched them, and looked at her fingers, astounded.

She touched Maddy's tears, and then she turned to the veil. To me, suspended in it, a part of the veil.

Aleena stepped up to the veil and slipped into it, joining me. She leaned down over my hands and touched my fingers to her face. I dissolved into her tears and fell to the ground, leaving Aleena in my place, a part of the veil.

CHAPTER TWELVE

THE ANCIENT BOY

I ONLY REMEMBERED BITS AFTER THAT. MADDY and Vivienne rolling me up in my cloak. Cawing all around me. Tugging at the cloth. A single caw, and then a rush of wings and a feeling of rising. Somehow I imagined my crows were lifting me. I was floating and then I was on Vivienne's back. Face in her fur, comforted by the musky smell, the soft warmth. My cloak tucking itself around me, gently cradling me, holding me tight so I wouldn't fall off.

From far away, I heard Brox saying, "Tell Keeper, and then find Greyfur and Eneirda." This was followed by a long caw from Corvus, and soft crow mutterings near my ear. Crowby. I smiled.

Then Maddy fussing, and Brox saying, "Carry him gently."

Swaying on Vivienne's back, and Vivienne singing. I couldn't make out the words, but it was something my mother sang when I was a baby. I let it carry me to sleep.

I woke in Keeper's arms as he lifted me down, stiff and aching. Keeper, Eneirda and Greyfur had set up camp at the base of Castle Mountain. They carried me to a bed of furs by a roaring fire, and insisted I drink and eat a little. Maddy hovered, refusing to eat until I did.

"We saw the other Greyfur and Reynar and Folens on the way back," said Maddy. "They were really worried about you, but oh, they looked so good. Strong and happy. Folens was giggling and playing."

I dreamed of Folens laughing.

For another day I dozed, only waking long enough to gag down the herbal concoctions Greyfur demanded I drink. Gradually, I began to feel better, but I could feel no magic. No magic, and not a hint of crowness, even when Crowby sat by me, murmuring softly. No magic in me, and no connection to the magic world. I felt unbearably sad.

But as I healed, the oranges and golds in the trees leaning over the river began to look particularly beautiful. Wrapped in my cloak, I lay in my nest of furs and dreamed of paint colours.

Brox healed faster than I did, as Eneirda and Greyfur

used herbs that Keeper collected to make a poultice for his crushed face. Vivienne sang to him as he rested on the grass, letting the herbs and their magic heal the damage.

Of course, nothing could rebuild his face or save his eye. The herbs and magic eased the pain and helped the torn skin and muscles knit, but the left side of his face was ruined. It was grotesquely ugly, but somehow beautiful, too. I wanted to sculpt that magnificent, scarred face.

When I was well enough, we told our story. Maddy and Brox did most of the talking, with Corvus interrupting and Vivienne correcting Brox. Crowby stood nearby, hopping at all the exciting parts.

When I described what had happened in the veil, Keeper said my dream was real, that Aleena had saved me with her tears.

A wave of grief swept over me. Keeper put his hand over mine. "Aleena learned to cry, to feel water. She would have been very happy."

As we sat in silence, remembering Aleena, the crows settled amoung us, a mass of black covering the ground. They stood completely still, totally quiet, honouring and mourning Aleena, their enemy. We sat with them until Corvus broke the silence with a single caw, and they rose in a black cloud, still utterly quiet.

Once they were circling and chattering again, Keeper called out, "Corvus, ask the crows to share the news. The Will of the Gathering is complete. The veil is rewoven."

The crows rejoiced, chortling and trilling, some doing barrel rolls over our heads. Then they scattered, only Corvus, Crowby and a few other crows staying behind, watching over me.

When it was quiet, I told Keeper, "I think it will be harder for magic folk to cross the veil, now. Not impossible, but harder. And I stranded magic folk and a girl and a tourist and some animals." I shook my head. "I'm sorry. I had to strengthen the veil."

Keeper nodded. "You did what was necessary."

"You can rescue them, can't you?" asked Maddy.

He smiled at her. "I will take care of them. But I am no longer Keeper."

Maddy frowned. "You *should* be Keeper. I know you destroyed the nexus ring, but you protect this whole land."

"You are much greater than the keeper of the ring," I said. "You're the keeper of the magic world."

Keeper stared down at me, his eyes wet. "That is what *you* are," he said. "I failed."

"No, you found me. I'm your magic boy," I said.

"You are the Ancient Boy."

"And you are Keeper."

"It is a good name," said Eneirda.

"It is a fine name," said Greyfur. "You were right about the human boy, *chrrr*. You have kept our world safe."

Keeper thought about it, and finally nodded. "Very well, I will still be Keeper."

Maddy grinned and leaned in for a hug. Then she looked at me. "Ancient Boy," she said, like she was trying on the name for size.

"Does it work?" I asked, "now that I'm back to normal?"

"Oh, you're not back to normal," she said, studying me. "You'll never be the way you were before."

"What do you mean?" I said. "My magic is gone."

"Maybe," she said. "But you're not just human any more."

VIVIENNE STOOD, HER FACE TURNED TO THE SKY. "A storm is coming. You need to return to Calgary."

Keeper stood, too. "Greyfur and Eneirda will take you."

"Are they well enough?" asked Maddy.

"Hnn, we are well now, thank you," said Eneirda.

They looked good, tall and joyful. I could see magic building in them again.

We wrapped our cloaks around ourselves.

"Children need to cross time, *tss,*" Eneirda reminded Keeper. "Josh will not be able to, and we cannot."

Corvus muttered, a low grumbly sentence. I muttered back and then I said, "The crows will help us.

Corvus says they'll be able to open the doorway and shift time."

"Even now, with the veil strengthened?" Keeper asked.

Maddy studied them. "Yes," she said. "They'll be fine. They're strong, together." Then she looked at me. "You can understand them?"

I stared at her, and then at Corvus. "Yes," I said, shocked. I listened to their chatter. "Yes, I can understand them now."

"You really are their crow boy," Maddy said.

I grinned, at Maddy and at the crows. I did have a little magic left, after all.

MADDY AND I STEPPED INTO THE BOAT WAITING for us on the shore of the Bow. Greyfur and Eneirda climbed in, and Crowby hopped onto the rim beside me.

Keeper wrapped magic around us.

"Our cloaks will keep us warm," I said.

He nodded. "Yes, and I will, too. You have done enough." He wrapped us in a bubble of warmth, Greyfur, Eneirda and Crowby, too. Crowby squawked and shook it off. Keeper grinned.

He pushed the boat into the river. The current was with us; it would be an easy trip home. Maddy called out goodbye and I waved. Keeper raised a hand in farewell.

The crows rose in a mass, cawing and trilling, chasing each other as they played in the sky.

Brox and Vivienne had left before us, slowly walking down the Bow, leaving the mountains for the winter. Vivienne led the way. As we floated past I could hear her singing:

Come, follow follow follow,
follow follow follow me.

My eyes lingered, wondering if we would be back. Then I looked at Keeper and the crows, and knew, absolutely, that we would be. We were part of this world.

As Greyfur and Eneirda paddled, Maddy and I began to sing:

My paddle's keen and bright,
flashing with silver,
swift as a wild goose flight,
dip, dip and swing.
Dip, dip and swing.

The songs Vivienne sings are old camp songs.

"Come Follow, Follow, Follow" (John Hilton, 1599-1657) is an old English round, but it may be more familiar in the version sung on *Sesame Street*, using the phrase "To the Redwood, Redwood Tree" (there are Redwood trees in California).

"Buffalo Gals" (John Hodges, 1844) and "Home on the Range" (adapted from the original by Dr. Brewster M. Higley, 1873) are American, and there are American versions of "Red River Valley," but it has been traced to Canada prior to 1886. "Land of the Silver Birch" is a traditional Canadian paddling song, and "My Paddle's Keen and Bright" is another paddling song (Margaret Embers McGee, 1918).

ACKNOWLEDGEMENTS

Thanks to the Alberta Foundation
for the Arts for financial support for this project.

Thanks again to Barbara Sapergia,
for her unerring eye, and to Rona Altrows,
for her steadfast encouragement.

Photograph by Mark Harding

ABOUT THE AUTHOR

MAUREEN BUSH is the author of five books for children, including the first two in the Veil of Magic series, The Nexus Ring and Crow Boy. Her books have been shortlisted for numerous awards, including the Silver Birch and the Saskatchewan Diamond Willow. Born in Edmonton, Maureen Bush now lives in Calgary with her husband and younger daughter.

Printed in Canada at Friesens